Cara Mia, My Darling

Jennifer Coulter Smith

authorHOUSE®

AuthorHouse™
1663 Liberty Drive
Bloomington, IN 47403
www.authorhouse.com
Phone: 1-800-839-8640

© 2009 Jennifer Coulter Smith. All rights reserved.

No part of this book may be reproduced, stored in a retrieval system, or transmitted by any means without the written permission of the author.

First published by AuthorHouse 7/21/2009

ISBN: 978-1-4490-0860-4 (e)
ISBN: 978-1-4490-0866-6 (sc)

Printed in the United States of America
Bloomington, Indiana

This book is printed on acid-free paper.

Dedication

I want to thank my husband, Greg, and my four children: Mary, Evan, Hank, and Seth, for putting up with me while writing this book. It has been a dream of mine for a long time to write a book and without you all I could not have done it.

I would also like to thank my Mom and Dad for pushing me to do my best and never give up on my dreams.

Chelsie, thank you for doing the tough work!

My 6th grade girls from Fredericktown Elementary School; you gave me ideas and encouraged me to keep going with this book! I will never forget you.

Last, I want to thank God. You placed this book and these characters right into my lap. I never had a day that I had to stop and wander what to write next. This truly was a gift from you that I will never forget.

CHAPTER 1
Mia and the Missing Link

I, Mia Brown, am what? Let's see, self-conscious and shy, yes! Too worried about what people think of me? Yes again! I really am just plain, plain, and more plain. I've always been the girl hiding in the background; always too shy to talk to almost anyone. And, I've never liked looking at myself in the mirror; because I don't want to see how plain I really am. I mean, come on, who sees straight sandy blonde hair, a pale complexion, and an average build as exquisite?

Maybe that is why, yet again, another guy has not called me after only one date. This happens to me every time I go out with someone. They want more than I am willing to give them and then they take off. *Well, I have morals and I will not change them for some man*, I thought to myself feeling mad and hurt at the same time.

Basically, I find it hard to be around adults, period. With all of the rejections from men, I feel like it is pointless to even try. My comfort zone is with kids, who are accepting and loving and have no negative thoughts or discriminations about me! They don't want anything from me that I can't give them. That's why I went into teaching. Although college had been a nightmare- the dreaded public speaking course was the worst- but I somehow had made it through.

I thought back to the day my professor, Mr. Kraft, pulled me aside one day after class and advised me to major in something that didn't involve speaking. He had stated very impolitely one day after giving a speech, "Mia darling, your voice is much too soft and shaky; it's like you've just ridden the scariest rollercoaster ever. Then there is the look on your face, it almost appeared to be seasick green," he added to the insult. I am glad that I didn't listen to him though, because I LOVE my job.

Well, so much for that teacher helping to build my self-confidence. Yes, I have been shy and self-conscious all of my life. Maybe if I hadn't been told these things about my personality so much from other people I wouldn't have started believing it myself. You know how it is, once you hear something so many times you start to believe it yourself. At one time or another, so many people have said to me, that I just needed to break out of my shell. I wish someone could show me just how to do that though....

"Ms. Brown, excuse me, Ms. Brown," a student interrupted my daydream about my boring and failed love life by tugging at my shirttail.

"Yes, Zoe, can I help you sweetie?" I asked the teary eyed five year old that stood before me.

"I want to go home," she whispered as her bottom lip quivered and her eyes welled up with big tears that were about to spill out over her eyes.

Draping my arm across her little shoulders I pulled her in to give her a hug. "Oh darling, we only have a little bit longer until Dad comes to pick you up," I promised.

It is the first few weeks of a brand-new school year that are the roughest for kindergarten students. Poor Zoe was having even a harder time than most of the class. Some students tend to leap into the school building full of energy and eagerness, while others came in more timid and scared. There are some who would just like to get to stay home; the safe place they had spent the first five years of their lives.

Something struck me about this child. Most little girls her age still get the sweet attention of their parents in the morning as they help them to dress and to fix their silky smooth hair. Some days the girls would come in with a neatly combed ponytail, other days donning a pair of cute dog-ears, still other days with their hair tucked behind a headband to keep it out of their eyes. This was not the case for Zoe, though. Every day since Kindergarten had begun exactly nine days ago she had come in with the same unruly ponytail setting at the base of her neck. She usually had on an outfit that looked pretty simple. It was basically a pair of cotton shorts and a solid color tee, along with a pair of plain white tennis shoes with pink shoelaces. Her little eyes always carried a sadness that was like a dark cloud covering her face. The only difference I ever saw in her from day to day was the color of her outfit.

She looked up at me again and had another question to ask, "What if he forgets to come and get me?"

"Oh honey, your daddy would never forget to come get you. He'll be here before you know it," I convinced her.

"OK," she stammered as she turned to head back to her seat at the round table in the back of the room.

That same afternoon I was pulled into the principal's office and found out why Zoe always seemed so sad and looked like her appearance was ignored. I discovered that day that my instincts were right about Zoe. Mrs. Brimlow, the principal at Cedar Creek Elementary, had asked me to come into her office after school to discuss an issue involving one of my students. When I walked into the office and saw not only the principal, but also the counselor, I knew it was going to be bad.

They explained to me that Zoe's mom was a free spirit. She was a private investigator and sometimes worked for the FBI on special cases. This followed serving for four years in the marine corp. When Zoe was one year old her mom had entered the marines and didn't get out until right when Zoe turned five. She had missed so many of this little girl's firsts; it seemed odd and sad at the same time. After returning home after a tour overseas in hostile territory, life seemed boring and mundane for this ex marine. That is why she decided to embark in a career as a private investigator. She went on mission after mission working for the government. At first, when she would go away she would call every night to tell Zoe goodnight and give her a kiss over the phone. She promised her that she loved her and would be home soon. It quickly started to dwindle, and the phone calls began to come but once a week, down to once a month, and eventually, the phone calls became very rare. Her last assignment was to find an escaped convict overseas and report his whereabouts. She boarded a jet that would take her to Africa and left Zoe and her father, Ben, watching and waving as she took off on her last journey. The mission proved deadly for her in the end. She was caught in crossfire she died doing what she believed she was meant to do. Ben had already told his daughter when her mom left that it was for work; she just couldn't be home for a while. When he got the notification that she had passed away he couldn't bear to think about telling his sweet little girl about it. Hours after getting the phone call he built up the courage to explain that Mommy wasn't coming home; that some bad people had hurt her and she'd gone to heaven. Zoe, too young to completely understand, went to bed crying wanting her mommy. Night after night Ben was the one having to live with the outbursts of tears and the questions that were left unanswered because he didn't know how to answer them. Zoe had wondered why her mommy didn't want her, why she didn't get to do things the other kids did with their mom's as well as other things. The end reality was that he would be raising a precious little bright-eyed girl by himself.

Sitting and listening to the principal, Mrs.Brilow, tell me about why this sweet little girl carried such sadness with her was almost unbearable for me. I had become very attached to Zoe in the short amount of time I had been her teacher, which is unusual for me. However, there are times in a person's life when they feel that Jesus is calling them to do something. This was one of those moments for me. I wanted so desperately to help Zoe, and to be able to fill the void that was in her life. But how could I somehow, just a teacher, be the missing link in her life?

Chapter 2

Ben's Hurt Continues

This school year has been flying by, yet things aren't getting any easier for me, I thought to myself as I pulled into the parking lot of Zoe's school where she'd started kindergarten eight months ago. I found myself still bitter at the fact that my wife had chosen to leave on a dangerous journey and had ended up with the fate I'd feared for all along. The funeral had been almost unbearable. Fighting my conflicting emotions like a grizzly bear would fight for its food, I had resigned myself to the fact that yes, a person can feel anger, hurt, regret, relief, and sadness all at the same time. How long would it take for all of these feelings to work themselves out? When would I ever begin to feel as if things were normal again? Maybe never, I thought as I brought my truck to a stop.

Yes, I had practically raised our daughter myself, but Laura was at least there some of the time before the accident. Now, I was alone, and that is a fact that I couldn't change. It was a bitter fact that I was having a hard time accepting. Before, I could at least talk about the time when Mom would be home and tell Zoe that Mom was doing important work to keep everyone here safe. But now, well, now I knew she would never be returning home to Zoe or myself.

"Give Dad a kiss." I lovingly spoke to my daughter as if she were the only person in the world worth loving.

Zoe gently hugged and kissed me, feeling the scratchy texture of my unshaven face. "*Ti Voglio Bene* Daddy. Until the stars all go away," she breathed into my ear. Having a strong Italian background, Zoe knew that those words meant "I love you daddy" and she used them often.

"*Ti Voglio Bene* Zoe, until the oceans dry up," I choked out, trying to hold back the well of tears forming in my smokey gray eyes. My daughter and I had always used these lines when telling each other goodbye, good night, or at any other time we wanted to show our love for one another.

She quickly bounded out of the blue Chevrolet truck I had bought about a year before the fateful accident. Laura had always thought it was silly buying such a big truck. I watched Zoe as she skipped into the building trying to act like she was happy. I looked after her until the doors of the school closed behind my precious daughter. I hurt because this sweet six-year-old girl felt that she had to be strong for me, like she needed to act like everything was okay.

I pulled out into the busy traffic, still thinking about my daughter's sweet kiss and soft words. I'd always been protective of her, but since Laura died it had become an even more intense instinct. I had decided in the past few months that all I needed to take care of from now on was Zoe and myself. I vowed never to fall in love again so that I wouldn't open up the possibility of getting hurt. I was just fine with Zoe and my restaurant and that was all I needed. Never again would I place the fate of my future in the hands of some woman. More importantly, I would never again let someone in Zoe's life who might end up crushing her just like her mother had done.

I drove out of town, away from the congested traffic and toward the restaurant I owned that lay just outside the city limits. Having grown up with both of my parents being chefs, I'd quickly developed a love for cooking. When my parents both fell ill after doing mission work in a small village in Africa they were left crippled from the illness and were left to live in the nursing home, not far from my log house outside of town. Since then I'd taken control of the restaurant and they had signed the ownership over to me, their son. At first I was nervous about running such a successful business. I'd been a chef at "The Stone Hallow Inn" for a couple of years prior to this but running a this popular restaurant on my own was a scary thought. Though my parents had a hard time talking I could tell by the bright look in their eyes that they were proud of me.

I jumped down out of my dirty truck after turning the engine off and strolled across the parking lot toward the stone building that looked like it could sit on a ranch resort in Montana. Large logs framed the double doors that led into the massive entryway where my prized trophy elk, deer, and bison hung. These were proof of my successful hunts from a more relaxed time in my life. I walked through the dining room and into the empty kitchen to get started on what I knew would be a busy lunch day. Fridays always seemed to be busy, but this Friday in particular I knew would prove to be even worse than normal. The State Education Convention was being held that Friday and Saturday in town and that always brought large crowds of hungry teachers and principals into the restaurant. I had received confirmation from the director of the association that they would need a buffet style lunch prepared for the group that day. This day would bring in some familiar faces from the past years: teachers from this town, and some new faces who I'd never met before. I always looked forward to seeing the many familiar and friendly faces but was worried that I would have to discuss the painful past year with the obviously concerned men and woman. I'd just wanted to try to put that part of my life behind me and start fresh, for Zoe's sake.

"Oh, I am going to throw this piece of junk out the window if it's the last thing I do," I impatiently ranted as someone walked in to the kitchen with out me even hardly noticing.

"Easy there Ben, don't be so eager to get rid of me," my long time friend Bo Winters said as he walked over to where I stood. "I just got back in town. Don't throw me out yet," he teased.

I turned to give my best friend a reassuring pat on the back. "Hey Bo, we've missed you this week. Did you have a good trip?" I questioned.

"Oh my, it was so peaceful and beautiful up there. It was just my boat, Lake Malone, and me. It was even better fishing than it was last year," he bragged. "Now, what is making you so mad that you are willing to throw it out the window?" Bo laughed.

Yes, most importantly Bo was my long time best friend, but he also prepared all the desserts for the restaurant. In addition to being a good cook, he was also a great handyman. The baking was acquired from growing up with four sisters. The handyman skills, he was just born with.

"You're not due back until Monday. I would hate to bother you, but if you are willing to offer, I will gladly accept some help," I pleaded. "This cappuccino machine is not working at all. I've tried everything but nothing seems to work," I said frustrated.

Bo got to work and after just five minutes of talking to me about his successful fishing trip his magical hands had the machine whirring to life as if it had just been pulled brand new from the box it came in.

Chapter 3
A Busy Day at the Restaurant

The morning passed quickly partly because I was so busy preparing lunch. Bo decided to stay until after lunch to help me out with the noon crowd. My curly black hair was damp from rushing around the hot kitchen. I could feel one curl lying loosely by my left eye and I took my tanned brown hand to quickly brush it away every now and then. I moved quickly from the hot stove to the counter and back in preparation of the feast I was preparing. Grace, my most dedicated hostess, was working that day. She entered into the kitchen and was enveloped by an aroma too good for words to describe.

"I hope we get to eat after the lunch crowd leaves. That lunch smells even better than normal," Grace declared while taking in the smell of rich prime rib and freshly caught rainbow trout.

Grace hadn't known me until coming to work at the restaurant but we had quickly become close friends. She almost seemed like a sister to me. It was easy for me to be friends with Grace. There was no tension or old ties that caused strain or stress. However, it was harder with Elly who is the other hostess. She had been Laura's long time best friend and every time I talked to her, or even looked at her, now all I could think about was Laura and the pain that she had caused both my daughter and me. Thankfully, she only worked weekends as a second job so I didn't have to run into her much. She was lifeguard at the local fitness and swim club in town during the week and just wanted to earn extra money on the weekend.

Getting back to the conversation with Grace I commented, "That depends on how hungry these teachers are." Of course I was just teasing her. I knew good and well that I'd fixed enough food for an army.

As the men and women started to file into the meeting room that adjoined the main dining room I thought that this afternoon would consist of overhearing teachers bragging about reading methods, dictating stories their students had written, or debating that math was the most useful and needed subject. It all sounded like a bunch of nonsense to me. However, I would smile politely and shake my head "yes" or "no" occasionally to act interested.

When everyone was seated the president of the association got up and gave a welcoming speech to the crowd who had joined him for the day. Peeking through the double doors at the crowd looking at the speaker most of them seemed as though they just wanted him to be quiet and wrap it up so they could eat. My eyes scanned the audience and saw a lot of familiar faces. Some were forcing smiles, while others were obviously eyeing the buffet line.

The speech was finally wrapped up after about five excruciating minutes. The speaker invited everyone to enjoy the elegant display of food before they went back to the nearby hotel conference center for sessions to begin. It looked like there were probably about fifty people in the crowd and they all lined up at the buffet and started to fill their white square plates that I had proudly chosen for the restaurant about a year ago. I frequently checked to see when anything was running low so that I could run to the kitchen and get refills. On my second trip out of the kitchen I made my way to the buffet line to refill the now empty roll container.

"Excuse me," I politely said to a blonde lady standing right in front of where I needed to get.

She looked around at me, eyes locking with mine, and scooted back out of my way. "Oh, I'm so sorry," she stated looking at me with sweet and caring eyes.

"Oh, hi Ms. Brown. You're fine, I just want to make sure everyone gets plenty of food, keep that buffet full," I admitted almost getting lost in her familiar blue eyes.

Why am I feeling this way? I know her, I thought to myself. It was my daughter's teacher, Mia Brown. I've seen her plenty of times and have never had this strange feeling before. I almost felt like I had tons of butterflies in the pit of my stomach.

I carefully placed the steaming rolls into the silver bowl that lay at the end of the buffet line. As I backed away I quickly glanced at Mia one more time, only to see her looking right back at me. I gave a small smile then quickly turned my head and headed back to the kitchen.

I thought about my conversation with my daughter this morning before school and did vaguely remember her saying she was going to have a substitute teacher today. I hadn't put two and two together and hadn't considered that Mia might be here at the restaurant today. But, why did it matter to me anyway? It was just my daughter's teacher, not my teenage crush.

"Hey, what's wrong Ben? You look like you are a thousand miles away right now," Bo commented as he saw me walk through the doors into the kitchen.

"Do what? Oh, nothing, Bo. I was just thinking about what a long morning it has been," I lied to my best friend. I was confused about the feelings I was having for Ms. Brown. Was I just feeling a connection because she taught my daughter or is it something else? It sure seemed like it was more than just that. All I knew was that no one else could know about these feelings that were being stirred up. The rest of the day, I tried to keep myself busy so that I wouldn't think about Mia's snow-white complexion and beautiful blue eyes. I pushed back thoughts about this woman every few minutes. I intentionally kept my eyes away from the table that she was sitting at every time I came out to refill one of the food trays. I knew the only things that I needed on my mind were my restaurant and my daughter. These two things kept me plenty busy and I had no room in my life for a woman who might just break my heart like my late wife. I just had to keep telling myself that.

Chapter 4

Good Food, Strange Feelings

"Mia, this is not a typical day of work," I said to myself as I walked to the buffet line at the Stone Hallow Inn. Friday's don't get much better than this, I thought as I stood in line at my favorite restaurant. I was away from the classroom for a day attending a conference and the luncheon was being held right here at the Stone Hallow Inn. I do love to teach my children, but it is nice to have a break every once in a while.

Feeling hungry and smelling delicious food, I found it hard to wait patiently in line. In fact, I was starting to understand how my students could get so antsy while waiting in line for something. The feast that lay out before me was invading my sense of smell. The Stone Hallow Inn had always been one of my favorite restaurants.

I found out just a week ago that this is where the convention would again be holding our buffet luncheon.

It had been here for the past fours years and I was glad that they chose it again this year.

I was getting close to the front of the line as I glanced up to see one of my student's fathers holding a plate of hot yeast rolls and walking toward the buffet to replace the plate that was now empty. I had forgotten that Zoe's dad owned and was the chef for this restaurant until I spotted him. She was probably one of the most innocent and sweet little girls I had ever taught. The only time I'd met with him this year was after the accidental death of Zoe's mother when we met to discuss the possibility of counseling for her. But, that had been a while ago toward the very beginning of the year. He seemed to have more of a sparkle in his eyes today than before. Cuter, suddenly came to mind, which was rather startling. Why did I notice he was cute and why did I care?

"I can't believe I am thinking that," I whispered to myself. I swear if I couldn't talk to myself I know I would be just lost. Teachers and students at school were use to my frequent conversations with myself and didn't even pay attention to me anymore.

I turned around and tried the, *I'll ignore him and not have to admit how cute he is*, tactic. About 15 seconds later I hear...

"Excuse me ma'am," coming from Ben's perfect lips.

"Oh, I am so sorry," I stammered, moving back out of his way. What was wrong with me?

"No, that's ok, I just didn't want to bump into you," he kind of whispered then, unlike when he'd first spoken.

Was he embarrassed that it was me, his daughter, Zoe's teacher? Did he not like me and decided to be as quiet as he could to avoid having to say much else? *Why do I even care* I thought?

His smile reminded me so much of his daughter; bright, wide, and stretching all the way across his darkened face. That is one thing I have always noticed about Zoe and her father, their dark complexion. The Italian blood was very apparent when looking at this daughter-father combo. His family had moved here from Italy when he was only five or six years old to start up a business, a restaurant. I had heard that it was now his, due to an accident or illness of his parents of some kind and that he was running the whole operation. You could tell family meant a lot to Zoe, too. She often wrote or drew about her dad and grandparents and how they cooked together and ate together every Sunday. I tried to imagine what it would be like to live around and hang with lots of family so often.

I again thought back to the time when I'd heard about his wife passing away earlier in the school year, almost right at the beginning. A sudden wave of sadness for this man swept throughout my body as I thought about him raising this little girl all by himself. All of a sudden it was like I could hear a voice deep inside of me telling me this man had been put in my life for a reason. Little Zoe didn't just end up in my class by accident this year. But why?

What was I suppose to do to help him? I know you are not supposed to question God when he opens doors for you or leads you somewhere unexpected, but what if I didn't know exactly where he was leading me? For some reason I had both a bad feeling in my stomach and a sense that I was in this place at this time to tell me that this man – Zoe's father - needed support. But how was I to be the one to give that to him?

Shaking off these strange feelings, I carried my full plate to the table of co-workers that I was with, sat down, and began to eat. I could hear everyone raving about how good the food was. I bit into my first forkful. No doubt, it was very good. Too bad the feeling in my stomach was going to keep me from eating much and from really enjoying it. I'd seen Ben many times, as I frequently came to this restaurant and had met with him a couple of times at school. However, I'd never had this strange flood of emotions overcome me. *So why now* I thought to myself.

"What's wrong Mia?" questioned Annie, my next door teaching partner. "You look like you just lost your favorite pair of shoes," she stated.

"Why does everything have to be compared to shoes, girl?" I laughed, avoiding her question.

"You know me, the queen of anything that goes on your feet," she responded truthfully. "But really, you seem distracted. Are you worried about your students being with a sub all day? They'll be okay you know. You're always thinking about school. You are dedicated, I'll give you that." Annie declared this like a news anchor relating a top news story.

"Yeah, just hope they aren't climbing the classroom wall." I laughed, knowing that was not what was really bothering me.

"Are you kidding me, your class? I highly doubt that," Annie remarked. She knew full well my class was the best-behaved in the whole school. "Just think you'll be back with your darlings on Monday."

I knew that, but somehow a whole weekend away from some of my students, notably one, seemed like a long time. "Yeah, and the weekend will go by so, so fast." I commented hopefully.

I continued eating, noticing I was having a hard time concentrating on the food on my plate. My mind and eyes kept wandering toward the kitchen where Ben was hidden. I was wondering why I couldn't get this get this tall, dark, and handsome man out of my mind. As I pictured his cute face, my own started to turn red like a tulip in full bloom. I had to make myself push those unnerving thoughts about this man, recently windowed, and worse than that the father of one of my students, out of my mind for good.

The afternoon passed slowly with meetings at the nearby convention center, which followed what had been one of the best tasting lunches I'd ever eaten. My stomach finally settled so that I could eat and I was stuffed when I walked out of the restaurant.

Thankfully, I'd had plenty to keep my mind busy so it wouldn't wander. The day came to an end and I trudged to my black Volvo and climbed in. I leaned back against the cool leather and put the key in the ignition. Immediately my car was filled with music. The sweet sound filled the air and my mind pushed all thoughts away. Finally, the weekend had begun and my mind could be distracted, at least for a little while.

Chapter 5

Shopping and Stressing

Opening my droopy eyes, I looked over at the clock blinking, not really registering what time it was. Then, I eyed my phone that had rudely taken me from a good dream. I rolled over and picked up the silver cordless phone off of my oak nightstand.

"Hello," I answered with a voice that was weaker than I meant for it to sound.

"Oh my, did I wake you?" I heard LeAnne, my best friend, asking me. "I thought you'd already be up getting ready for church," she apologized.

"I can't believe it is this late! I must have hit the alarm clock and then gone back to sleep, I am so glad you called me," I thanked her. "Church in one hour and I still need to take a shower," I whined, knowing that meant that I'd have to rush, and I hate to rush.

"Well, I was just going to see if you'd like to go shopping with me today after church" LeAnne offered. "I need some new spring clothes and I have a wedding in a couple of weeks that I need to get a new dress for," she explained.

"Like you need an excuse to go shopping," I joked. LeAnne would take any excuse at all to be able to go shopping. "Sure, it sounds like fun. I actually don't have a thing to do today anyway," I commented knowing maybe that going out shopping would be a good distraction for me. "But, I am only going to go if ...," I began.

"I know, if we eat out," she finished. That was usually the highlight of our shopping trips. We both loved getting to set down, eat a good meal, and have some girl talk. Being with kids all week, I felt like I needed some adult time.

I laughed at LeAnne. She could almost always finish my sentences for me. We had been best friends since second grade and had been two peas in a pod while growing up. We dressed alike, thought alike, and even ate the same foods. I once heard that to be truly happy in life you need three things, one of those being good friends. Well, LeAnne definitely fits the bill there! Now if only I could get the other two: good family, and accepting who I am and where I am in my life. I think if I could find that special person to marry and spend the rest of my life with it would help me reach a level of satisfaction that I haven't yet been able to find. Of course, I also want children of my own one day.

Cara Mia, My Darling

I got off the phone after LeAnne and I agreed that we'd meet after church and ride in her car to the mall. I crawled out of bed, feeling a little more chipper now than when I first awoke. If there is anyone who can make me smile and make me believe that I could be happy with someone some day it was LeAnne. Knowing that I'd be spending the day with her brightened my mood significantly!

I took a quick shower and after I dried my hair only partially I threw it in a ponytail. I put on just enough make-up to as least look like I was awake, chose a comfy but suitable outfit for church to put on, and then headed out the door. I looked at my reflection in the glass of the storm door as it shut and nodded approvingly at the khaki capri pants, pink polo shirt, and brown sandals that I had put on. I was excited that I got to pull out my warm weather clothes! April 21st, and this was the first day that it was warm enough for sandals- my favorite foot attire.

That Sunday church seemed a little shorter than normal. St.Paul's, in downtown Oak Ridge, had a priest visiting while our normal pastor was away on a retreat. Father Blair fit right in with everyone, and he was always the one who took Father Jim's place when he was away. The gospel and sermon for that Sunday had really made me think about my own life.

So Jacob worked seven years to pay for Rachel. But his love for her was so strong that it seemed to him but a few days. Genesis 29:20

So, why can't I have a love like that I wondered? Isn't it what God meant for me? I sometimes wondered if God had wanted me to be with someone, to have a love like Rachel had or is the path that God chose for me to be by myself. I tried to live my life, as He wants me to and to trust that He will take care of me. Well, I sometimes wonder why things are like they are and what exactly my mission in life is.

I listened to the spectacular choir at church. They had such angelic voices that seemed to rise up to Heaven. I would have loved to join them, to stand proud and sing the songs of faith. But, with my shy personality I would never try it. My family always said that I could sing pretty well. But, that was not enough to coax me into getting up on that altar and singing in front of so many people every week. I just followed along with the crowd, tucked into my little pew where I wouldn't have to worry about the possibility of fainting from embarrassment or fright.

The choir finished the beautiful rendition of *"Amazing Grace"* and the congregation quietly headed toward the back of the church and out the tall oak doors to the porch. When I got outside I spotted LeAnne waiting for me at the bottom of the steps.

"Hey, were you in church?" I asked my friend as I walked up to her and looked at her perfect hair and clothes. She was always the picture of beauty; even in her workout clothes she was gorgeous. She didn't have to work for this beauty. In fact, she didn't wear much make-up at all. She had the kind of natural beauty that is rare. The sad thing is she doesn't even see it. She thinks she is just as plain as I am.

"Yeah, you were the one to get up late but I was the one to get to church late. I just sat in the back," she explained.

"Well, I say let's get this shopping trip underway," I spoke excitedly walking toward the parking lot.

We had to drive a little over a half an hour to get to the nearest mall. By myself that would have been a boring trip, but with LeAnne it was magnificent. Her Red Toyota Avalon was filled with relaxed conversation the whole way there. The discussion included our summer plans, talk about her little girl and what we needed to purchase while we were at the mall.

"So, are you going to Louisville for the fireworks this weekend?" LeAnne asked me, even though she knew that I never went.

I shot her a knowing look, "You know I always stay home and watch it on TV. I don't have a sweetie to curl up next to on a blanket and watch them with," I reminded her. LeAnne and Mike had gone every year to Thunder Over Louisville, the annual Derby Festival Event for the past 6 years that they had been together. That is where Mike had proposed to her during their junior year in college. They were married one year later, and within 6 months they were expecting their first child. Their sweet little Danielle is the joy of their lives. I longed to have a daughter or son that would look at me the way LeAnne's daughter looked at her.

"You ought to come. We have room on our blanket and Danielle would love to have you come with us," she kept after me.

"I don't know, I think I'd rather stay away from the crowds," I responded. I had never liked being around a lot of people. The Kentucky Derby events drew thousands of spectators, so they are not places for a shy out of place woman to be.

We pulled into the parking lot of the humongous mall, a girl's paradise. There were so many stores inside that I could never get to them all in one shopping trip. I had my route down pat, though. First, I would browse through the clothes at my favorite two stores; then on to whichever shoe store is having the biggest sale. After that, I will stop and go get some of the best smelling lotions around, which help make bath time a luxurious experience. Finally, I'll end up at the book store. I always end my shopping trips by choosing a new romance novel or a suspense story that will keep me on edge. Reading is my favorite way to pass time, and being single with no kids I had plenty of free time to read. I always had a little while to get started on my new book before LeAnne would catch up with me. She takes shopping very seriously and never gets in a rush when trying to find the best bargains.

Today's trip followed my normal course of action to the tee. I first purchased two new pairs of capris for work and three new tops (blue, pink, and yellow). I love buying new spring and summer clothes, because they are so bright and cheery. Then, my weakness took over. I bought six new pairs of flip flops and two pair of sandals. I cannot seem to fight my attraction with shoes anymore than a puppy can resist chewing on a bone. To my defense, the shoe store was having a buy one get one half off sale. My next stop landed me two bottles of lotion, one country apple and the other mango. Then, it was on to the bookstore where I got two books instead of the usual one. Both were romance books that would remind me of what I didn't have, I was prepared for that already though.

Just then, a strange thought popped into my head. It wasn't the realization of how much money I had spent, although I had spent a lot. It was Ben. I had been able to push thoughts of him away for the entire weekend, but now thinking about what was written on the pages of these books made the thoughts and funny feelings about him come back again. The thoughts weren't uneasy because he was a bad person or because I didn't like him. It was that I was his daughter's teacher and that he had just been recently widowed. That would be crossing a line I shouldn't cross in both cases. I am sure he was still severely mourning the loss of Zoe's mom, his wife. I had to find a way to get my mind off of that man, and fast.

"Hey LeAnne, did you buy the store out?" I joked as I saw her coming toward me lugging bag after bag in her arms.

She laughed. "No, I left a few items for others." she said teasing me. "I do know I have worked up an appetite though. Are you ready to eat?"

"Thought you'd never ask," I admitted.

"Where do you want to eat?" I asked her. She always chose the same Mexican restaurant but I asked anyway.

"Let's eat somewhere different this time," LeAnne answered.

"Really? I thought for sure it would be another chicken enchilada bake weekend. What's made you sway from your normal choice of restaurant?" I questioned her.

LeAnne responded, "I just thought a steak and hot potato sounded good for a change.

Hearing her recommendation of food I noticed my stomach start to fill with butterflies. Feeling like a teenager again. I waited nervously to hear her restaurant choice, knowing what it was going to be.

"Let's splurge and go to Stone Hallow Inn," LeAnne suggested. "I know it's a little more expensive than what we normally do, but I haven't eaten out for two weeks, and I think that makes me deserving of a treat," she said grinning from ear to ear.

"Oh, well, yeah okay. I just ate lunch there Friday at my meeting, but if you want to I guess that'll be ok." I stammered over her words.

"What's wrong, you act like I suggested going to the back alley to eat. I thought you loved Stone Hallow Inn. If

I do recall I think I believe you once said they had the best steaks within a 100 mile radius," LeAnne said teasingly.

"Yeah, I do like it. Let's go. I was just surprised that you changed your mind from your usual choice, that's all," I commented. *Oh my gosh*, I thought. *I am trying to get this man out of my mind and Leanne wants to go, of all places, his restaurants.*

We walked to the car, climbed in after getting our bags stuffed in the trunk, and started off for lunch. I was going to have to find a way to keep LeAnne from seeing my nervousness.

We pulled up to the stone building, parked, and started toward the front door.

Chapter 6

Stone Hallow Inn

We walked through the front doors and into the restaurant. As always the first two things I noticed were the trophy game on wall and the smells of delicious food.

We were taken to our seat in a booth on the outside wall by a young, friendly hostess. I looked outside at the sun setting in the western sky. It really was a beautiful night with hints of pink and purple painted along the horizon. I always did think that a beautiful sunset was a gift of art from God

"You're waiter will be with you in just a moment," the hostess assured us.

"Thank you," we said in unison.

We both picked up our menus and started to scan the large selection of appetizers and main entrees. I finally decided on a house salad, barbeque pork chops and a baked sweet potato. LeAnne chose the chicken fried steak, mashed potatoes and green beans. We looked up to see a dark, handsome man with curly dark hair standing over us. I was almost frozen. Was our waiter really going to be none other than Ben Allegra?

"Good evening ladies, can I get your drink orders?" he asked in a deep husky voice.

I struggled to get the words out finally able to say, "Sweet tea please."

LeAnne added, "Same for me."

"I'll be right back with your drinks then," Ben said smiling a pearl white smile at both of us before heading off toward the kitchen.

LeAnne looked wide eyed at me. "What was that Mia? You looked like you were going to pass out or something. Do you know him? What am I missing?" she rambled on.

"He is the owner and chef of this place," I explained. "and, I teach his daughter."

"She must be a little monster to evoke that kind of response from you," LeAnne guessed.

"Oh no, on the contrary; I think I could take her home with me. She's one of the sweetest kids I have every taught," I said kind of in a daze.

"Then what... oh, you must..., is he married?" she tried to ask so many questions at once.

"No, he is widowed," I began and went on to tell her the story about his wife. His angelic face interrupted us when he came to give us our drinks. LeAnne and I asked for a few more minutes to look over the menu, really just needing more time to talk about him.

"So, do you like him? That would explain the reaction you had to him," she guessed.

"No," I began. "Well, I mean I can't," I finally spat out sounding frustrated.

Ben walked back over to our seats, "Are you two fine ladies ready to place your orders now?"

My heart was beating out of my chest like a teenager who had a crush on the senior quarterback. I had to admit to myself I was attracted to him. But, like the shy teen with a crush on the quarterback, I had no choice but to deny myself of even thinking about it because my chances with him would be slim to none. Plus, I taught his daughter which again might be weird.

Somehow, I managed to get my order out to him, though I thought LeAnne might break out into a fit of laughter before he left our table. She ordered her meal and he walked toward the kitchen to place our orders.

"I am going to get you," I hissed, slapping her arm. "He probably thinks we are crazy after that."

LeAnne, now seeing he was a safe enough distance away, broke out into a full-blown laugh. She finally calmed down enough to tell me I reminded her of a little schoolgirl with a crush on her teacher.

"Okay LeAnne, that is enough," I cautioned her. I don't want ANYONE to know how I feel. I'd be humiliated, so just forget about my feelings toward him, please," I begged her. Then I teased her saying, "You being my best friend would make it harder on me when I had to hurt you if you spilled the beans."

"First of all, Mia, I am your oldest friend and I would never hurt you. But, don't think I am going to let this go. He might be the one: your happily ever after. And Mia, you haven't dated in forever," she urged.

"I teach his daughter. It be totally uncomfortable. Also, I would have no chance with a guy that looks like a model who just stepped off the runway," I went on. "Plus, he just lost his wife in a horrible tragedy 9 months ago. Don't you think that would be too soon?"

"First of all, so what if you're her teacher? It will be for what, another couple of months? Don't give me that line that you wouldn't have a chance," she continued. "I bet he'd love to have a mother figure in his daughter's life. You know it has to be hard raising that little girl on his own. And, I bet he thinks you are prettier than what you think, Mia. You just don't see it do you?" she added.

I could tell LeAnne was not going to let this drop easily. Ben headed toward our table balancing a round tray on his hand with two plates of food for my friend and me.

"I hope you two enjoy your meal," he remarked. "I would hate for you to have to admit to Zoe at school that her daddy can't cook," he teased looking right at me.

I am going to faint, I thought to myself. "Oh, I have never had a meal here that I didn't like," I assured him.

"Why thank you for the lovely compliment Ms. Brown," he commented.

"Oh my, no, please call me Mia," I insisted. "Ms. Brown makes me sound old."

"Mia! Well, that is a lovely name. I will have to remember that, I definitely not want to make you feel old," he promised.

"Thank you," I said blushing as he turned to walk off.

I had forgotten that LeAnne was even there when she spoke."Earth to Mia! Are you still here with me?" LeAnne joked. "Did you forget that I was here?" she asked me.

"Of course not," I lied to her in a less than convincing manner.

My friend continued, "I believe he might have an eye for you too."

"Yeah right," I doubted, but wished that she was right.

LeAnne and I finished the rest of our dinner by arguing our cases for and against my trying to flirt with Ben. I knew my best friend was stubborn and I knew she wanted me to be happy. In this situation, both of these factors really worried me.

After dinner, LeAnne drove me back to the church to pick up my car. I watched her drive off toward her house, where there was a waiting husband and baby girl. A twang of jealousy surged through my veins and I wished that I was doing the same thing. I however, would be going home to an empty house. My night would consist of playing with my cat and snuggling with a pillow to help me fall asleep.

On my way home I was sure of one thing: that tonight my dreams would be filled with the most perfect man I had ever met.

Chapter 7

I Am Not A Waiter

I know I'm not waiter. I am the owner, operator, and chef of a hugely popular restaurant, but not a waiter. So, why on this Sunday at suppertime did I find myself telling the usual waitress for table twelve that I'd get that table for her tonight since her load was full? Was I an idiot? Won't I be hurt when I get turned down by the girl that I seemed to be so attracted to?

"Hey Rachel, I've got table twelve, you look like your hands are full, dear," I had commented just minutes ago.

"Thanks Ben, I am kind of swamped," she said in a strange voice, wondering why I had the sudden urge to help out the waitresses.

I could try to deny it, I could pretend I was just being helpful. In fact, I would probably convince my waitress that I was just trying to help out. However, deep down I knew I saw that woman, Mia Brown, as much more than just a customer to wait on. I had been trying to push back feelings I'd been having about her since the day of the education convention at the restaurant. These feelings were one's I hadn't felt in quite some time, or maybe had ever felt. New, strange, uncontrollable feelings. I knew my wife had just died about eight and a half months before, but she had been away for months and months before the accident even happened. I had never really felt as if I were married because she always left me so alone. Still, it hit when she died and I knew that my little girl would feel the effects of her death for a long time. Besides, I sat and vowed just a few months ago that I would never let a woman into my life again. So what in the world was I doing?

I couldn't believe that I was doing this. I was on my way to table twelve with a pad of paper and pen in hand to take Ms. Brown's order along with the young lady she was eating with. Inside I was shaking like a leaf while on the outside I had to keep telling myself to remain calm.

As I approached their table a sudden wave of confidence coursed through my body. I got their drink orders and eventually food orders without showing how I was feeling inside. It was the most exhilarating sensation! After Mia had left I still found my mind drifting back to her and seeing her sparkling blue eyes that looked like they had so much caring and compassion in them. I knew she was aware about what happened to Laura. I was just thankful she hadn't brought it up. I would like to try to move on from that painful part of my life- make a fresh start. And,

I knew I wanted that fresh start to included Mia Brown, no matter what I had said about not letting anyone else into my heart. It was like some supernatural force pushing us together. Before Friday I'd barely known she existed except for seeing her now and then at Zoe's school. I just hoped she didn't see me as a single father with too much baggage to deal with.

That night I closed up the restaurant, cleaned up, and headed out to my truck to drive home. I was looking forward to Monday, the day of the week I always took a break and closed down the restaurant. A cleaning crew came in on Mondays and made sure the place was spotless. On this Monday in particular, I was going to go to Zoe's school to have lunch with her. She had been asking me for quite some time, and I hated to disappoint my daughter.

I exited the busy highway and turned onto the much calmer Windy Branch Lane where I'd lived the past 4 years. I thought about what I was going to go do tomorrow, how I would act at the school, and if I would get to see or talk to Mia Brown. I had basically made up my mind that I had been alone long enough and that being with Mia was the best opportunity I'd had in a long time. She was a sweet, caring, and compassionate woman. Obviously she was wonderful with kids and that is what Zoe needed; a mother figure in her life. The thought of rejection weighed in the back of my mind but not enough to keep me from going after what I thought was meant to be.

I pulled into my driveway and turned the engine to my truck off. After I paid the babysitter and let her out, I crept up the stairs to peek in at Zoe. She was sleeping peacefully, curled up in her bed and hugging the teddy bear she got when she turned one year old. I can't remember a night since then that she hasn't slept with that rugged old bear. I was glad she had it, though. It helped to comfort her. I felt so guilty at times for leaving her with a babysitter so much. I really didn't have much choice though, with the restaurant. *Hopefully*, I thought, *one day I'll get married again and Zoe will have a step-mom who will be able to stay with her at night, go to PTO meetings and make a good life for her.*

Mia fit that description as well as the description of the woman I believed could make me happy.

Chapter 8

Why Me?

I awoke on Monday morning to the rude sound of my alarm clocking beeping away. My mind automatically went back to my supper with LeAnne the night before. I had never been so excited and nervous at the same time. Never having been being a dater in high school I missed a lot of those heart-breaking times.

"I can't believe it is already Monday morning," I said to myself as I climbed out of my warm bed to face the morning. I looked out of the window beside my bed to see a dismal cloudy gray sky and rain pouring down.

"Oh, have you ever! Monday morning is bad enough let alone adding the rain to it," I complained to my cat Snowball. Can't I just stay at home, curl back up into my bed, and read all day?" I asked my distracted cat who was trying to catch a fly buzzing around his head. "Oh great, now you don't even care if I am here or not," I teased him as I trudged off toward my bathroom.

I entered, hesitated, and then flipped on the switch. It filled my enormous cherry colored bathroom with a yellowish light. I drug myself to the shower and climbed in. When I turned the water on I was immediately surrounded by a hot cloud of steam as the waterfall drifted over my tired shoulders. The shopping had worn my legs out more than I had realized. I started to feel my senses come to life, thanks to the smell of my lavender soap and beads of water hitting my back.

"Maybe today won't be so bad," I said out loud to my self as I began to wake up.

Snowball, now interested and wanting my attention, sat on the rug by the shower as I stepped out to dry off.

"Meow," Snowball added to the conversation that I was having with myself.

I bent over after drying off and putting on a big tee shirt and scooped my cat into my arms. He snuggled into my lap and drifted off to sleep as I sat at the counter and applied my make-up. I've never been one to wear much make-up, so it didn't take me too long to put it on. I pulled my long blonde hair into a ponytail and left the bathroom- placing Snowball back on my bed.

I walked down the short hallway into the kitchen just as the phone on the wall rang.

"Hello," I answered, already knowing it was Mom from the caller id.

"Hey, Mia, how are you this Monday morning honey?" my mom asked from her end of the line in sunny Florida. Mom and Dad moved to Florida after they retired. It had been something they wanted to do all their lives.

"Hey, Mom. Well, it's Monday morning and it is raining cats and dogs outside. Does that answer how I am?" I trailed off, getting depressed all over again.

"You need to come visit us in Florida, Mia, get you some sun and sand," This was Mom's usual response.

"Well, Mom," I began, "some people have to work for a living, remember," I joked with her.

"Yes, dear, I do remember. But, you know your dad and I have said we'd buy you an airline ticket to come visit one weekend. Come in on a Friday and stay until Sunday afternoon. That would be a nice long weekend," was her response.

"I know Mom. One day in the next couple of months I plan to take you up on that. Okay," I promised.

"Well, I'm going to hold you to that," she said. "I am in desperate need of a hug and kiss from my beautiful daughter," she added sweetly.

"OK Mom. But only you would call me beautiful," I mumbled.

"What was that Mia? I can't understand you," my mom asked.

"Oh, nothing, Mom. I will come down soon, I promise. I love you and dad but I have to go get ready for work now," I told her.

"I love you too, baby doll. Can't wait to see you," she spoke lovingly into the phone.

Sometimes I wonder what she thinks of me. Here I am, Mom and Dad's only daughter, and I am not even married. It will be quite some time before they will have a chance of getting grandchildren, at least from me. She has to be ashamed of me. My brother, who is two years younger than me, is married and already has a baby girl.

"Ughh, just stop it Mia," I told myself. You are going to make yourself more depressed than you already are.

I got my coffee going and went back into my room to get dressed for work. I chose a simple pair of khaki pants, my pink polo shirt with the school name on the pocket, and a pair of hiking boots to wade through the water with. After dressing I headed back into the kitchen to grab my coffee and keys before heading out the door for work.

I tried to say some prayers on my way to work. I prayed to God to send a good, wholesome, honest man into my life. A man who would make me complete. It seemed like all the guys I'd ever gone out with wanted one thing from me, and when they find out I am waiting until marriage to give them that part of me they are instantly gone.

I want someone who shares the same values I have or at least respects me for what I want. I want a man who is caring, sweet, good with children, will help around the house some, and respect me. Of course, it wouldn't hurt for him to be tall, dark, and handsome too, I thought to myself. I knew I just described my perfect man- though I doubted a guy existed that met each criteria I listed. I did have a certain chef, a father of a sweet little girl, coming into my mind, though. But why?

The three-mile drive through the tree lined downtown to work was quick as usual. Cars and trucks were lining up in the parking lot to drop their children off for school that Monday morning.

I parked in my assigned parking spot, got out, and started walking toward the school with my umbrella in hand to try and keep dry. Today I was wondering why my parking spot couldn't be close to the front doors.

I entered the building and walked into the office where the school secretary greeted me.

"Good morning Ms. Brown," she spoke softly.

"Good morning Mrs. Shane," I answered back. "It sure is a nasty day out there today, isn't it," I commented on the weather.

"It sure is," she said back.

I started to walk toward the door that leads to the hallway when Mrs. Shane stopped me.

"Oh, wait just a minute Ms. Brown," Mrs. Shane said. "You have a phone message."

"Oh really, thanks a lot. But if it's a mad parent then no thanks," I said laughing. I took the note from her hands and wondered what it could be about. I unfolded the crease of the note and began to read. My eyes got wider and my heart started to race. *Oh my goodness, Ben is coming to eat lunch with Zoe today.* I instinctively looked down at what

I was wearing hoping I looked pretty decent. I thought I was way to plain. I wondered to myself why I couldn't stand out from every other woman at least just to him. The fact that I even cared what I looked like and wanted him to notice me told me my heart was going to a place it really shouldn't go.

I walked toward my classroom in a trance, knowing I was going to have to pull it together. People would soon start to wonder what was up with me if I couldn't talk right and stared into space constantly. If I could pull off looking cool, calm, and collected, with the way I was feeling, I should have won Academy Award for it.

Thankfully, when I got to my classroom there was a room full of Kindergarteners there waiting for me. Usually, I am not so eager to see them, but this morning I needed a distraction. For the most part, the morning went well and the class were able to keep me occupied. However, every time I looked at Zoe my heart would start to flutter and I would get butterflies in my stomach.

"OK, boys and girls, lets have a seat, " I commanded to the rowdy roomful of kids.

They all started to head to their own little seats as I walked to the calendar at the front of the room.

"Now, how did you all like the substitute that was here on Friday?" I questioned them.

"Oh, we missed you Ms. Brown," all the students shouted, although they did say they really liked Ms. Janes, the substitute.

"Well good, and I missed you all too," I told the class. "Now, tell me, who had a really good weekend," I asked next.

"Me, me, me," I heard the students around the room say.

Zoe raised her hand really high into the air. It looked like she wanted to tell me something very important.

"Yes dear, what do you need to tell me?" I asked her. This was a very strange occurrence. Zoe hardly ever spoke out in class or raised her hand to speak. She was usually very quiet and didn't volunteer to say much.

"Yes, Ms. Brown, I have something really exciting from this weekend," she spoke in a slightly more upbeat voice than usual, although still very quiet.

"Well Zoe, what has you so excited this morning?" I asked her.

"My dad told me last night that he would come eat lunch with me today," Zoe spoke in an excited and loving voice. It was so sweet to see her look forward to something so much.

I on the other hand got a funny feeling in my stomach and it did a little flip at the sound of her talking about her father. I smiled down toward her excited freckle face not knowing exactly what to say to her.

"Great Zoe, I am glad you are so happy about that," I finally mustered to get out. That was all I could manage to say though afraid I might show my nervousness about this little girls handsome father coming into our classroom today. My cheeks grew hot and red thinking about this intriguing man and I decided I'd better get on with calendar time so that I could make it until lunch without melting.

The rest of the morning went by fairly fast and smooth. I looked at the clock and it was 11:03, only two minutes until lunch. *Oh my gosh*, I thought, *I could feel my stomach start to know up like a school girl going to recess anxious to see her crush.* I thought to myself *that if my stomach didn't settle down I might not be able to eat any of my lunch.*

"Okay class, let's all go wash our hands and line up for lunch", I instructed.

Once everyone was in line with clean hands I opened up the door to the hallway nervous of who might be standing outside. I led the class quietly to the cafeteria door, beginning to think he was just waiting in the cafeteria for his daughter and I wouldn't have to run into him at all. Not that I didn't want to see him. It would just be easier to accept that I didn't have a chance with him if I told myself that, rather than getting turned down by him personally.

Why was I doing this to myself? I thought. *I have to stop beating up on myself and have more confidence in myself.*

I glanced at Zoe who stood at the end of the line looking around for her dad, who was the reason she'd been smiling all morning. Just then, I saw Zoe look toward the end of the hall. Her eyes lit up and she took off running into the open and waiting arms of her father. Nothing could have taken the place of the look in that girl's eyes when she saw her father standing and waiting for her.

"Daddy, you came!" Zoe said in an excited voice.

"Of course I did, sweetheart. But you'd better not run, or Ms. Brown might get you," he said looking in my direction and smiling, revealing the dimples in each of his cheeks.

As his eyes met mine I felt as though I might faint. I smiled back at him as he walked up to me and said hello.

"Hi, Mr. Allegra. I hope you know you have made one little girl's day by coming to eat lunch with her today," I said, trying to make easy conversation before I got tongue tied and couldn't talk at all.

"Yes, I can tell she is a little excited. She could hardly get to sleep last night for thinking about today. She'd been asking me all year but I have just been so swamped that I am just now getting a change to come," Ben said. "But, what is this "Mr. Allegra"? You thought Ms. Brown made you sound old, so what makes you think I want to be called Mr. Allegra?" he questioned me while continuing to smile.

"Ok, Ben," I said to him mockingly. "Is that better?"

"Yes ma'am," he answered and winked.

I couldn't help but think that his wink was just one of friendliness. I also thought about how that this man was going to have a hard time fulfilling his duties as father as well as operating and cooking for his restaurant. I couldn't help but feel sorry for him. He had dealt with more than a person should have to.

By this point I had almost forgotten the students were still standing in line waiting for me to let them into the cafeteria. I twisted quickly to tell the class to go on in for lunch and hurt my ankle in the process.

"Ow," I bit my lip to try and forget the pain in my ankle. I reach out for the wall to brace myself, but had a strong hand grab me instead.

"Woah, are you okay," Ben asked as he used his arms to keep me upright. I felt like I would fall over right then. Which would be ok if it were him that would be catching me.

"I am the clumsiest person on the face of this Earth," I said honestly. "I can't walk for tripping over lines, now I guess I can't turn without twisting my ankle.

"Let's get you to the office and sit you down so someone can take a look at that ankle," he urged, giving me a slight nudge.

"No, no, I'll be fine. Like I said, I am really clumsy, so I am used to hurting myself. It'll be ok in a few minutes. I just need to shake it off," I said.

He started to protest, but I stopped him before he could say a word.

"No, we're not arguing here," I stated flatly. "You have an excited little girl waiting to eat lunch with her daddy and you aren't going to disappoint her now. Okay?"

"Yes ma'am," he said again with a grin. " I know better than to argue with a teacher, especially one that seems very stubborn," he declared, laughing lightly now.

I couldn't help but flash a wide smile at him. My eyes followed him and his daughter into the lunchroom where they joined the lunch line. I could still feel his strong hands at my waist holding me up. I knew at that moment I was falling hard for this man. The question was, who would be there to pick me up when I hit the ground. I knew that it would happen when he turned away and rejected me?

Chapter 9

A Visit From Mom

The rest of the week seemed to pass by very quickly. Before I knew it, Friday afternoon was here again. I didn't have any plans, and I came in from work and saw the answering machine light blinking. I walked over and pushed play only to hear my dear mother's voice speaking to me.

"Mia, honey, it's your mom. Since you haven't been able to come home since Christmas, and, with school, might be too busy to come for a while, I am coming up to Kentucky to see you. I will be in on the five o'clock flight and will just take a cab in from there, I don't want to put you out to come get me. Love you and see you soon," the answering machine went off after my mother finished her speech.

I looked at my watch; it read three forty-five. I thought to myself that I was not going to make my mom take a cab in when I could just go pick her up. It had been a while since we'd had a good talk, and I needed one of those right then.

I picked my purse, keys, and phone back up and headed to my room to change into something more comfortable. I grabbed an orange for a snack and headed back out the door to go pick up my mom. The rain had stopped by then and the sun was starting to make its first appearance of the day as it edged out from behind a big cloud. It was such a nice and quiet ride to the airport, and it seemed as if I was there in no time.

I pulled into the parking garage and wondered if I'd find a spot to park. Glancing at my watch, I saw that it was four forty-five. Just fifteen minutes and my mom's plane was do to arrive. Finally, after parking my pearl white Ford Escape next to the fifth level stairs, I got out into the dark shadows of the level the parking garage. I have never like parking in these places. It felt as if eyes were watching me from behind every shadowy corner. I started down the narrow staircase and entered the double doors that led to the main lobby. I quickly checked to see which gate my mom would be coming through . The flashing red sign confirmed what the attendant had told me, Flight 123 from Atlanta, Georgia, would be getting off at gate fourteen. I found an oversized blue seat facing the runway to sit in while waiting for the plane to come. After about five minutes I spotted the Delta 727 landing on the runway and coming to a stop. It took about ten minutes before Mom got off the plane and walked through the door at the gate where I was waiting for her.

"Well for heaven's sake Sweet Girl, what are you doing here? I really could have taken a cab to your place," my mother said while hugging me tightly. "Have you lost weight child? You need to eat and put some meat on those bones," she commented next.

That's my mother, always worrying about me taking care of myself, especially since they moved away and I was living on my own.

"Mom, I weigh the same I did a year ago and the same as a couple of months ago when we saw each other last. You just worry too much!" I told her.

"Well, you could still handle some food, and I'm hungry from the trip," she complained.

"What do you want to eat?" I asked her.

"How about a steak at Stone Hallow Inn," she suggested.

"Oh, we don't have to eat anywhere fancy on my account Mom. What about a burger at McDonald's or something?" I asked her.

"You aren't having money trouble are you sweetie?" she replied.

"No, Mom. I am not having money troubles." I answered her not wanting to tell her the real reason for not wanting to go to that particular restaurant.

"Honey, it's one of my favorite places to go when I come home. Now, take your old visiting mother to the restaurant of her choice," she teased me.

"Okay, we'll go there." I gave in knowing there was no use arguing with her.

My mom and I talked the whole way to the restaurant. She caught me up with what had been going on with her, Dad, and their new friends in Florida. I told her about the how the school year had been going and how much I loved the group kindergartners that I had that year. When we arrived and pulled into the parking lot I parked, opened my door, and began to panic. I opened her door slowly for her and asked again if she was sure she wanted to eat here.

"Why are you acting so strange Mia?" my mom asked.

I commented, "I'm fine, just tired from a long day at work and want to make sure this will make you happy."

"Well, gracious child, you act like you've seen a ghost, you are so fidgety," she chided.

I laughed, knowing how my mom liked to over dramatize things.

When we walked in, we were greeted by a pretty brunette who seated us very close to where LeAnne and I had eaten just a little while before. I nervously eyed the double doors to see which waiter or waitress we were going to get.

Mom noticed, "Is there something you are looking for?"

"No, just looking around," I lied to my mom for the second time in less than a half an hour.

"Oh my, is there a young man here, is that why you've been acting so strange?" she asked knowing I wasn't good at hiding anything.

"No mom, are you just crazy anymore? You try to set me up with someone every time you come visit," I complained trying to turn the conversation in a different direction.

"Well, if you would just start dating on your own I wouldn't have to go looking for you, now would I Sweet Darling?" she continued.

Rolling my eyes and looking back down at the menu I saw a figure moving in our direction from the corner of my eyes. I was so thankful our waitress was coming so that the conversation would, hopefully, drop. I looked up ready to place my order and froze.

"*Cara Mia*, may I help you?" Ben questioned my mom and me smiling.

I am going to faint, I just know it, I thought to myself. *Why do I always have to be placed in these types of situations? He is so handsome. And look at the muscles in his arms showing through the tee shirt that hugs him like a glove.* I looked into his smoky eyes even though I'd told myself I shouldn't. He was staring right at me. How would

I fool my mother now, the one who can see right through me?

"Can I have just a few more minutes?" my mom blurted out before I could say a word.

"Sure thing Mrs. . . . ." he stammered.

"Oh, its Mrs. Brown, Mia's mother," she said confirming to him that I was definitely not married.

"Well, it is nice to meet the mother of such a fine teacher," he complimented. "And to think, I wondered if you were her sister," he said as he turned to give us some more time. He glanced back and added, "Mia, I hope the ankle is okay now,"

"Yes, it's fine thanks," I answered, lying because it was a bit sore.

"I think I might blush, thinking I was your sister," my mother said as he walked away. "And look at that behind he has, my goodness it is as firm as...," she was saying as I interrupted her.

"Mom, come on, what are you doing? I knew you were going to embarrass me tonight," I whined to her hoping she would stop before he overheard one of her comments about him, no matter how true they might be.

"Mia Brown, I could tell by that exchange there is something going on there. Now, spill the beans. And what is wrong with your ankle?" she asked, demanding to know the answer.

"There is nothing going on Mom, honest. I teach his child and when he was at school today eating lunch with her I twisted my ankle," I said, trying to ease her crawl.

"Then why, if he is just a parent, does it seem as if I've missed something? From the look on your face when he walked up to the table I would say there is more to it," she observed.

Why did my mother have to see me so clearly? "You are just imagining things, Mom," I assured her.

"Is he married?" I was asked next.

Thankfully, at that moment, Ben came back to take our orders.

"Ready, ladies?" he questioned.

"Yes," we said in unison.

We placed our orders and Ben took off, probably to cook the food orders he had just taken. *He must either really be a multi-tasker or he needs help around here bad*, I assumed.

"Now, answer my question," Mom resumed the conversation from where it had left off.

I proceeded to tell her the whole story about how Ben's wife had gotten killed and he was raising Zoe on his own. I summed up the whole story into about five minutes.

"He sure is cute." She wasn't going to let this drop.

Ben returned to the table to bring our drinks. As he handed me my glass his hand gently touched the side of mine. A hot flame shot through my hand and into the rest of my body. I wondered if he felt the electricity that was there. I looked at his face to read his expression. He smiled a gentle smile at me as he spoke, "Excuse me."

"Oh, that's okay," I smiled back, fighting my shyness.

He handed my mom her drink and turned to head back to the kitchen.

"Oh my gosh," my mom stated, jaw dropping. "I saw that!"

"Don't Mom, it's not going to go anywhere," I warned her.

"Why Mia?" she demanded. "You two obviously have some chemistry between you," she said.

"No Mom, he is very nice, and I will admit he is cute," I said. "But, I teach his daughter and he is getting over the death of his wife."

Mom looked hesitantly at me. I could see she wanted to be stubborn and continue, but she knew that I was just as stubborn as she was.

"Okay. I came to visit you, not to nose into your personal life. Or your lack of a personal life, either," She stated.

I flashed her a dirty look for that last comment and quickly changed the subject. We talked all through dinner about everything but Ben. I couldn't help but notice my mom's expression every time he came to the table.

We left the restaurant after a delicious meal and eventually some good conversation. I got my mother to my house, got her settle in, and went to bed. Deep down I knew there was no chance of sleep for me for a while that night. I simply could not get my mind off of Ben, or what my mom had apparently noticed at supper. This one time in my life I hoped my mother was right. I hoped that the spark that I felt, Ben felt too.

Chapter 10

Could It Be?

After an exhausting day of preparing dishes for the people who came in the restaurant, I closed up and began to clean the kitchen area. About an hour after close, I finally climbed into my truck and took off for home where I would be able to see my sweet Zoe sound asleep in her little princess bed.

My mind was so distracted that I barely even noticed a deer dart out in front of me. Slamming on the breaks, I was jolted back into reality, and thankfully missed the huge buck that, had I been hunting, would have tried with all my might to catch.

"I have to get my mind on the road before I have a wreck," I said aloud to myself. It was an internal struggle to try to do that however. My mind kept drifting back to Mia at the restaurant earlier that night; how sweet and caring she seemed to be.

When I pulled into my driveway, I could tell the lights in Zoe's bedroom were off. Only a small nightlight shined any light through her upstairs window. I walked up to the door, turned the lock, and walked inside to the foyer. *This deafening silence is too much*, I thought to myself as I leaned over to turn on the radio with the remote control. Immediately I was greeted with the sounds of Beethoven and Bach. Others always thought I was strange but I couldn't help but love classical music.

"Mrs. Parker, I'm home," I called out to our elderly neighbor who kept Zoe on Friday and Saturday nights since they are my late nights.

"In here, dear," she answered from the kitchen. *There is no doubt she is in there cleaning up something. The poor thing never quits or rests when she is here; even though I have told her over and over to*, I thought as I walked toward where she was.

Walking into the kitchen, I gave the sweet old lady a gentle hug. She reminded me so much of my own grandmother, who had passed away just a couple of years ago. The soft white hair, the wrinkles around her eyes and mouth; it all just reminded me of the hard work the many years of her life.

"Do you want me to take you home tonight, Mrs. Parker?" I asked.

"Oh my, no dear. I can walk across the yard and be home in just two minutes," she promised me. "It'll do these old bones good to get some exercise," she admitted.

That woman amazed me. She was 78 years old and still got around like it was nothing.

"If you are sure," I said to her, knowing not to argue. "How was Zoe tonight?" I asked.

"Sweet as ever! She just needs a mom in her life so bad. I can tell by comments she makes that she misses the mother-daughter things she sees her friends doing with their moms," she told me.

"Yeah, me too," I admitted. My mind immediately went back to the restaurant tonight and the beautiful Mia, Brown. I really think God placed this lovely, gentle flower in my life for a reason. I could tell from the couple of times I'd seen Ms. Brown that it would be up to me to make the first move. She seemed very shy and reserved. I decided that I would have to see if there was a future for us, or if I was just having a silly teenage crush on this woman?

"Well, Ben, you're as cute as a button. I tell you what, when you want to start dating again the girls will line up for you," Mrs. Parker stated grinning, a toothy smile at me.

I thought about how, there was just one girl I could think of that I wanted to be in my life, to fill that void in my daughter's life. I didn't need lots of women lining up at my door wanting to date, I only needed one.

"Thanks Mrs. Parker, for everything you do," I said to her giving her another hug and a twenty dollar bill, which is all she would allow me to pay her.

"Oh Honey, I don't have grandchildren so this works out just as good for me as it does you," she insisted. "Good night."

"Night," I said back to Mrs. Parker. I watched her walk across the yard and into her own house. The big wooden door shut behind her and I turned and headed toward the staircase to go look in on Zoe.

As I got to the top of the stairs I heard a rumble of thunder outside as a spring storm made itself known. I looked into Zoe's room, and laying sound asleep under the pink and white bedspread was the angel that I had been raising for the last few years on my own. She looked so beautiful in her flowery pajamas and soft dark curls falling over her pillow. She needed a mom in her life like the flowers outside needed the rain. The worries and thoughts she had to deal with were more than a six year old little girl should have to deal with.

I thought back to the marriage that Laura and I had shared, or rather, not shared. Though we had been married for quite some time before the accident ever happened we had never really had a true marriage. She had spent more time overseas than at home with Zoe and myself. I wanted more than anything else to find a woman to marry that could be home with Zoe every night to help her with her homework. I wanted a woman who would braid her hair for school and put her in little dresses for church. Lastly, I wanted something I had hardly ever had; a woman who was there to lie beside me in bed at night and listen to my problems I had or share my joys. In some ways I was sad that I'd never had that with Laura. But, the fact was, that I knew that it wasn't a real part of our lives and it made not having her there now a little easier. Could the part of me that was finally moving on want to move ahead with Mia? I wasn't quite sure yet. All I knew was that she made me have feelings that I'd never even felt for Laura. She made me smile, and made me weak in the knees when I saw her. I knew what I had to do, and I didn't plan on taking long to jump into action.

As I climbed into bed after showering, tired from a long day of work, I said my prayers. As usual the prayers included my business, parents, my daughter, and good health. Most recently, though, I had added something to my list that sometimes I though was too much to ask God for; that was to bring a good woman into my life who could make me happy and be a good mom to my daughter. That night my prayers were a little different though, tonight I thanked God for opening up a door that might include Mia in it.

As I fell asleep I had a dream, a very good, detailed dream. Mia was standing at the foot of my staircase, kneeling down next to Zoe. She had one arm around my daughter and one holding a little baby; the baby I knew was ours. I could vaguely remember how happy Zoe had looked in the dream, I was almost sad when I woke up the next morning, because the dream was over. My new mission had now become clear: to make my dreams come true.

Cara Mia, My Darling

I climbed out of bed before I really wanted to, but knew Zoe would be out of bed very soon, wanting something to eat. As I entered the kitchen in my tee shirt and shorts my daughter came running and flung herself into my arms.

"Good morning, Sweet Pea," I spoke lovingly as I wrapped her up in my strong arms.

"Hi, Daddy! Do I get to stay home with you today?" she asked, stretching her arms over her head.

"Yes Sweetie, its cartoon day," I told her, then went on to add that it was also Daddy and Zoe day. On Saturdays I didn't go into work until late afternoon so that I could spend as much time with Zoe as possible.

"Do you have to go to work tonight, Daddy?" Zoe asked, almost as if she had been reading my mind.

"Yes honey, but I don't have to be there until five o'clock tonight. How does that sound?" I asked her.

"Yay! Can we do something then?" she wondered, knowing there weren't many Saturdays that were this nice and that I didn't have to go in to work earlier than five.

"Well, that depends. What would you like to do?" I questioned.

"Shopping!" she spoke excitedly about her favorite pastime.

"Oh girl, I wasn't ready for you to become such a little shopper this early in your life," I teased her, laughing.

"Daddy!" Zoe begged.

"Okay, we'll have breakfast and then go for a little while," I gave in to the puppy dog eyes and pouty face.

"What kind of breakfast would you like for me to fix you?" I wondered.

"Pancakes," she said, as if I didn't know what her choice would be.

"Okay, pancakes it is," I spoke. I continued to go about the kitchen getting the pancake batter, mixed up, and on the griddle. I fixed her heart shaped pancakes that morning after adding fresh blueberries to the mix. We both sat down to enjoy the blueberry pancakes and a big glass of chocolate milk. I talked to her about lots of different things that morning, eventually making our way to the topic of school.

"So Zoe, how do you like your teacher at school?" I asked her.

"I love her Daddy; she is the nicest person I know. Oh, except for you, of course," she corrected herself, seeing my hurt face. "And she's really pretty too, Daddy," Zoe added.

"That's sweet honey, a good save," I teased. "Would you like to have her over for supper sometime?" I asked her, trying to get a feel for how she would react.

That thought must have almost been too much for Zoe because she almost leapt into my lap. "Really daddy, we can really get her to come here for supper?" she asked me. "I can't wait! When is she coming?" Zoe prodded me to get information.

I started to think that I shouldn't have brought this up so prematurely.

"Well, Zoe, I don't know if she will or not. I thought first I might ask her to come to the restaurant and have supper with me first one night," I told her. "Then if we get along, well, she can come to our house," I finished.

"Oh okay," she said at first sounding disappointed. But, she must have thought about what I said because then she perked up and said, "Wow, does that mean she is going to be your girlfriend, Daddy?"

"Slow down Zoe, I just want to get to know her better. She seems like a really nice person, and would like to get to spend some time with her," I clarified, before she got her hopes up too much.

Zoe calmed down after that and finished her pancakes. After I'd cleaned up the dishes and straightened the kitchen up I got her clothes changed and put her hair up in a ponytail. We headed to the garage and piled into the truck.

The next thing I knew we were pulling up to the shopping center. I parked as close as I could and got out holding Zoe's hand while we crossed the parking lot.

"Where first, Zoe?" I asked her.

"Can we go to the shoe store?" she asked. I should have known that was coming, with her passion for shoes.

"Alright then, off we go then," I announced looking to see which direction we needed to go to get to the shoe store. As we entered through the front doors, Zoe burst loose from my hands and took off through the store by herself.

"Zoe Maria Allegra, get back here," I shouted after her not wanting her to get out of my sight.

I looked up to see Zoe running toward her teacher, Mia.

"Ms. Brown, what are you doing here?" she squealed in delight.

As I approached the two I found myself going into father mode. "Zoe, don't you ever run off from me like that again."

"Ben, I am so sorry. She saw me and took off before I could let her know that I would walk over to see her," Mia apologized.

"No, that's ok. She should know better than to run off from me," I assured her.

"I'm sorry, Daddy, but I saw Ms. Brown and didn't want her to leave before I got to talk to her," Zoe apologized with her brown eyes full of sadness and regret.

I knelt down next to her and wrapped my arms around her tiny waist. "Honey, I just don't want anything to happen to you. Promise you won't do it again," I told her.

"Okay daddy, I won't," Zoe promised before looking up at Mia again. "Guess what, Ms. Brown? You get to come to my house and eat supper one day after you eat with Daddy first at the restaurant so he can make sure that you will like him first," Zoe rambled on and I jumped in to stop her.

"Zoe," I exclaimed feeling as if I might crawl under the nearest rock or into a deep hole. I didn't know what else to say, looking at Mia who was a more than just a little puzzled. "Can't you keep a secret little girl?" I asked to her.

Turning, I looked directly at Mia and tried to explain what Zoe had blurted out. "Mia, I am so sorry. This morning at breakfast I asked Zoe if she would like for you to come eat supper one night at our house, I wanted to make sure she wouldn't be nervous for her teacher to come over," I said blushing a bright red. At this point I knew God didn't want me to back out on my plan. And, since Zoe had so unexpectedly helped to get my plan going by squealing to Mia I figured I should continue, "I was thinking first though that maybe you'd like to come to the Stone Hallow Inn for supper as my guest one night," I suggested, not sure if the invitation sounded right or not since I had to come up with a way to ask her on the spot.

Mia must have thought it was okay, though, because she quickly accepted my invitation. "Yes, I would love to," Mia answered. "It is my favorite restaurant," she added.

"Okay, how about Thursday night?" I asked, not knowing if that was too soon or not.

"Sure, sounds great. That will be one night I don't have to worry about fixing supper for just myself," she said.

"Can I come?" Zoe jumped into the conversation.

"No, honey, that is a school night. You'd better stay home with Mrs. Parker," I told her.

"Aw, Dad. What about the next time?" she whined.

I laughed, seeing that the question was a little premature. "We'll see Zoe, we'll see," I answered hoping that there would be a next time.

Zoe and I told Mia goodbye and we went our separate ways; Zoe and I to the shoes and Mia to the checkout lines.

The excitement I felt at that moment was more than I could have imagined. I felt I could have kissed Zoe for wanting to come shopping, Zoe blurting my plans out wasn't how I'd planned on asking Mia out, but the result was exactly what I'd hoped for.

CHAPTER 11

Finally, 6 O'clock

This has been the longest week of my life. Having to wait from Sunday, the day I got asked out by Ben; until Thursday, which is when we had our date planned, is horrible. All I could think about was what to wear, what would we talk about, and would I be too nervous to eat the food he was preparing for me?

I had told LeAnne about my "date" that same afternoon that I saw Ben and Zoe at the mall. I was like a teenager that had just been asked to her first prom. She was so excited for me. But, her reaction was nothing compared to that of my mother's. I wish I could have had her response on tape.

"Praise the Lord, miracles do still happen!" she exclaimed.

Poor Mom, she wanted to see me happily married with kids, which is very sweet. Sometimes though, she could drive me insane about it. It's not like I carry a sign saying "guys go away" or anything. Every relationship I'd had with a guy in the last three years had ended in the same way within three dates. I always got dumped or I walked away from the relationship because I was not willing to give up the part of me that should wait until marriage. I strongly believed in abstinence when one was single, but now, there weren't many people that share that belief. I heard every excuse in the book on why I should give in to my feelings and forget my beliefs. I always had the same answer waiting for anything that was thrown at me though; no. I believe it is supposed to be that way and I would not give in just to please a guy. God tried to lead us down the right path in life. I prefer to keep going in the direction he led us in as much as possible.

I wasn't supposed to meet Ben at his restaurant until six but I could hardly wait. I got in the shower at one o'clock, got ready as soon as I got out of the shower, and then sat on my couch and looked at my cat. The clock still only said three. What would I do for three hours? I got up and looked in the full length mirror three times, checking to see that I had on the right outfit, and each time decided that I just looked okay. I chose a pair of jeans and a pink and brown button up shirt. I picked out a pair of brown sandals to finish the outfit off.

Next, I decided to go get on the Internet and check my emails. It had been so long since I'd checked it that I figured I would have so much junk to go through it might take two or three hours. I logged on and started sorting through the emails. I was putting what I needed in the "keep" pile and the ones I didn't need I was sending to the "trash" pile, the latter being the fullest. After going through three hundred and forty two emails I was left with only forty-six that were worth keeping. One of the emails that I had saved was from my best friend. It was a blonde joke which she always loved to pass on. Also, my principal had emailed about needing volunteers for a luncheon the next week, and I had an email from my cousin in Ohio. When I opened it up, I read that she was getting married. She had gotten engaged that weekend before and wanted to ask me to be in the wedding. It was going to be a Christmas wedding, December 19th. Go figure. I was always the bridesmaid and never the bride. All of my cousins were leaving me in the single world all alone to fend for myself. *Maybe Ben won't leave me there too long, though-* wow, I had to stop myself. "Getting a little ahead of yourself, don't ya think Mia?" I said out loud.

I glanced up at the brown wall where the big clock hung and jumped up in disbelief.

"Oh my goodness, it's time to go," I yelled out to Snowball as I grabbed my purse and jumped to my feet. I leaned over and gave my cat a quick pat on the back and told her to wish me good luck. With that, I closed the door to my house and walked to my car. I could tell my hands were starting to shake even before I had trouble getting the keys in the ignition. Finally, I had the car started and was on my way. I thought nervously over and over again how the night might go. I played scene after scene over in my head until I pulled into the parking lot of the Stone Hallow Inn restaurant. There weren't nearly the amount of people here on a Thursday night as there usually is when I am here on the weekends.

I slowly got out of my car and walked nervously and excitedly toward the massive building and quickly noticed the silhouette of a man standing near the front door. The figure began to open the door as I approached. As he stepped into the light I saw that it was Ben, and felt a surge of relief run through my mind.

"*Cara Mia.* How are you this evening?" he questioned me with a slightly heavier Italian accent than usual.

"I am wonderful! How are you?" I asked back. When he spoke to me in Italian saying, *Cara Mia,* I couldn't help but wonder what it meant.

"Wonderful! I have been looking forward to our dinner tonight. Would you like to take a tour of the kitchen, see where I create my masterpieces?" He asked me with an heir of cockiness.

"Sure, I feel special getting the grand tour and a meal from the master chef himself," I teased back.

Surprisingly, he took one of my hands into his and led me to the double doors at the back of the restaurant. As he pushed to open the doors my eyes took in the sight of a world class, high-tech kitchen.

"Wow, this is amazing," I exclaimed in awe. "I have never quite seen a set up like this before. Do you ever get tired of cooking in this kitchen?" I asked him.

"It does get a little overwhelming at times. Sometimes it is easier to just cook in my little kitchen at home. One stove, one sink, and only two people to cook for," he answered me back.

"Miss Zoe is one lucky little girl to have a chef as a dad. I'll bet she is never disappointed at what you put in front of her at meal time," I guessed.

"Well, she is a kid, so there are times when she isn't completely thrilled with what I put on the table. Mealtime is important to us though. When I was a small child in Italy I can remember that was the most important time of the day. We all sat together every night and talked about the events from the day. I would like to carry on that tradition with my daughter. Of course the conversation right now at the dinner table is pretty simplistic," he stated. "Sometimes I do get to hear about school though. She even mentions her teacher every now and then," he said smiling and winking at me.

"Oh, that scares me. I hope I don't sound like a horrible monster to you," I admitted.

"On the contrary, she is quite fond of you," he told me.

I continued to look around the kitchen at the shiny stainless steel pots and pans, the humongous ovens, and the walk in fridge that was as big as my whole kitchen.

"Being in this kitchen and smelling this delicious food is making me hungry. What are we going to have tonight for supper?" I asked him.

"Well, how does eggplant parmesan, a Caesar salad, and cheesecake to wrap it all up for dessert sound?" he asked me.

"My mouth is already watering," I had to admit, hearing the delicious menu planned for tonight.

Again he took my hand and led me back into the dining room where there were even less people than when I had entered the kitchen just ten minutes before. He led me to a corner where it was romantically low lit and surrounded by plants. He pulled a chair out for me and I sat down. Walking around to the chair next to me he sat down. Our arms rested merely inches away from each other.

"I am going to let one of my waitresses take care of us tonight so that I can sit and talk to you," he said, thinking about the last two times I was here when he'd been my waiter.

"That sounds great," I said softly.

"Ok, Ms. Brown, tell me a little about yourself," he said, seeming legitimately interested in what I would say.

I told him about growing up as a shy child with my parents, and about how they moved away to Florida after they retired. Next, I told him about my love of children and how I decided to go into teaching. I went on to talk about other tidbits of information about me, but not wanting to say too much.

"That's basically all," I finished just a short time later.

"Now come on Mia, there has to be more than that," he prodded me for more details about my life.

"Not really, I've had a pretty boring life. I guess that could be bad in some people's eyes, but I personally think it is a good thing," I stated.

"That's true, but I just have a feeling there's more to you than just what you've told me," he stated as he winked at me. Our dinner came out and we began eating, and continued some light conversation.

After eating for a while I said, reminding him, "I don't believe you've told me anything about you yet."

He grinned a sly grin, like he was about to do something that would get him into trouble. "Well, Mia, do you really want to know all about me?"

"Yes sir, I would like to know what Ben Allegra is all about," I answered him in a teasingly mocking voice.

"Well," he started, "I have a six year old daughter who is in kindergarten," he smiled.

"Oh, aren't I getting deep and dark secrets out of you?" I teased him. "That is information I am sure no one knows about," I said sarcastically.

"Well, I have to say, there is one more thing that is very interesting," he teased talking very slowly.

"And what would that be, Mr. Man of Mystery? Am I going to find out something that is so top secret that only the government would know about it?" I asked him jokingly.

"It's better than that, it is something that no one knows about," he teased. Leaning in closer to me as if he were really going to tell me a juicy secret he whispered into my ear. "The best part is that my daughter's teacher is a really sweet, honest, and beautiful person," he finished, looking deeply into my eyes with a smile that was both flirty and honest at the same time.

I felt my cheeks burning with heat and my heart was pounding so hard I could swear he'd hear it. "She sounds wonderful," I breathed out in merely a whisper wanting to see if he was going to say anything else.

"Yeah, I hope I get a chance to get to know her a lot better," he admitted, still so close it was scary. "You wouldn't happen to know how I could get in touch with her to let her know this do you?" he asked in a husky voice.

"I happen to know her very well," I went on.

"Do you think she would give me a chance and spend some time getting to know each other better," he asked.

"I'd almost guarantee she will," I answered, then added, "she'd be crazy not to."

He went back to his side of the table smiling a very sweet and sexy smile. Settling back into his chair he began to eat the food that was still on his plate. I also finished eating, and neither one of us said anything else for a few minutes.

"This was absolutely delicious Ben," I complimented him, breaking the silence that filled the air.

"Thank you very much, it is what I enjoy doing. However, in my opinion, the company was as enjoyable as the food," he said sweetly. He reached across the table and took my hand in his. "Listen, Mia. I have really enjoyed tonight. I don't know what it is, but I feel so comfortable around you, like I've know you forever," he admitted.

Almost speechless, I searched my mind for the right words to say, "I have had a really nice time too," I finally stated, not knowing what else to say, and feeling the electricity between us.

"Do you think we could get together soon?" he asked her.

"Sure, I would love that," I answered him, trying to downplay my enthusiasm a little bit.

"Great. Actually, I have to admit I've already talked to Zoe about the possibility of having you over for supper, I hope your not mad," he batted his dark eyelashes at me.

It did seem a little quick and presumptuous but how could I get mad with those puppy do eyes staring at me like that. "No, not mad, just shocked I guess."

"Why?" he asked me.

"Because I've never had a guy be such a gentleman to me before. And, it just seems soon to come eat at your house," I admitted.

"First, I will always treat you with respect like a gentleman should. Number two, Zoe loves you, and I've had a crush on you for a few weeks now," he finally admitted to her.

For the second time tonight I started to blush. I was happy and shy about the whole situation. The only words I could get out were that I didn't know what to say.

"You don't have to say anything else," he added as if reading my mind.

"Yes, of course," I said.

Ben stood up to take my hand and helped me up.

He walked me out to my car quietly. Turning to face me, Ben, leaned in closely, allowing me to take in the musky smell of his cologne. He placed a soft, gentle kiss on my right cheek, then my left, and whispered in my ear, "Until the next time *Cara Mia*." He then turned and walked back into the restaurant, leaving my heart beating fast, and feeling totally breathless.

Chapter 12

Falling Hard

I awoke the next morning to beautiful sunlight streaming through my bedside window and across my queen-sized bed. It was finally the weekend, and I had so much to do. I needed to clean my dirty house that I had let go for way too long. I also could stand to go to the grocery, considering I'd had cereal for supper the past two nights. I also needed to get a start on next week's lesson plans, although with the end of the year nearing the plans are considerably easier than earlier in the year.

Wow, I still can't believe the school year is just about gone, I thought to myself as I sat up and stretched my arms over my head. Snowball bounced up into bed with me and curled onto my lap showing the love that he had for me.

Yesterday had been the longest day of my year, so far. My mind kept wandering back to the restaurant and how wonderful a time I had with Ben on Thursday night. I wondered, quite often, if he had enjoyed it as much as I had and if he was thinking of me. I couldn't help but think that he too, felt the immediate attraction that was between the two of us. The conversation flowed as smoothly as if we'd known each other forever.

I was snapped back into reality when Snowball stood up and licked my cheek, meowing to tell me it was time for him to eat. I leaned back and eyed the phone, wanting so much to call Ben and just see how his Friday went. He had told me on Thursday night that I could call anytime and that he'd love to get together again really soon. Before I knew what I was doing, my hand had picked up the receiver and started dialing the number. Within two rings I heard a voice on the other end of the phone answer with a chipper "hello".

As I was hearing his voice I started to panic. *Why had I done this* I thought? We had been out on one date and why did I feel like I could just call to check in and say "hey". Even worse than that I was calling on a Saturday morning at 8:30 am, and he or Zoe could have still been in bed.

I hesitated and then answered him back, "Good morning Ben. How are you doing this morning?"

"I am wonderful, my Dear. And how is the charming Ms. Brown doing this Saturday morning?" he asked me.

"Great, thank you! I know it's early, but I remember hearing you say that some Saturdays you like to get up, beat the heat, and take your dog out for a walk. I was just getting ready to get up and go for a walk myself and thought I would see if you and Zoe would like to come along with me and you could take Mr. Boots along us too," I said hoping I didn't sound as nervous as I felt.

"How nice of you, Mia," he commented. "I have to take Zoe to soccer practice at ten thirty. Are you getting ready to go now?" he asked knowing he would have to finish in time to get Zoe home, changed, and back to the soccer field.

"Yes, I was going to be leaving my house within the next fifteen minutes. All I have to do is throw my hair up, put on my walking clothes, and down a quick cup of coffee," I said.

"Do you want me to pick you up on the way to the park?" he asked me.

"Well, actually, I always just walk to the park from my house. It's only about a half mile and the traffic this time of the morning is really light," I suggested, liking the extra exercise time.

"Ok, that'll be great. Is there a sidewalk the whole way to the park? Zoe would love to ride her bike there," he noted.

"Oh yeah, it is a great flat path that goes right to the entrance of the park," I answered him.

"Okay then, count us in, we will be over in just a few minutes. I'll just have to throw her bike in the back of my truck to bring over. Where exactly do you live?" he asked me.

"I am at 423 Rockwood Drive. You'll take a right onto my road just after you pass the city limit sign," I directed him. "I have a simple one story house, cream siding, front porch with a rocking chair and a swing. One of the few distinguishing aspects of my house is the concrete pig that sits just below my flagpole. I know it sounds silly but I love pigs and when I saw it at the nursery last year I just had to get it," I explained.

Laughing, he said, "Interesting but helpful information. I am sure to find you now with the help of the pig. I will see you in a few minutes, Mia."

"Okay, I'll be ready," I answered and hung up the receiver of the phone. "I can't believe I just did that," I screamed aloud in the emptiness of my house. *I am usually so shy and would never call a man. What has gotten into me?* I must be completely crazy I thought to myself thinking that might be a possibility. *I've really only known this man for a week and now I am calling him up to go to the park with me. Oh my gosh, I have lost my mind.* I can't believe *this man is already pulling on emotions that I have never felt before and causing me to do things that I never thought I would do.* I thought feeling like I was going crazy.

All of the sudden I thought about the fact that I was still in my pajamas and Ben would be walking through my door with his daughter in the next ten to fifteen minutes. I frantically jumped up and ran to the bathroom. I threw open the closet door that held my collection of clothes and picked out something that I could feel comfortable walking in and still look pretty good. It was a little cool that morning, so I chose a pair of black yoga pants with a pink stripe going down the side of the leg. Next, I tossed on a pink tee shirt with the word Pilates written across it that I got from a class I took a couple of years ago over my sports bra. I grabbed a pair of socks and my walking shoes and sat on the bed to put them on. I went into the bathroom, threw my long hair into a ponytail, and applied just enough powder to my face so that it might cover up some of my imperfections. After I looked in the mirror, only half pleased with the way I looked, I walked to my living room to wait at the door for Ben and Zoe.

As I was entering the living room I saw movement through my front window followed by a knock on the front door. It had to be Ben. I opened up the door as I was saying good morning to Ben and stopped. It was the mailman, Charlie. He had a box that wouldn't fit in my mailbox so he brought it to the door.

"Hey, Charlie. How are you today?" I asked, disappointed that it wasn't Ben standing there.

"He laughed and answered, "Well, I am okay but I assume you were expecting someone else from the look on your face," he guessed.

"Thank you for bringing the mail up, but yes I have a friend coming over to go walking with me. But, it is always nice to get to talk to my favorite mailman," I said honestly to the sweet man who had been delivering mail in my town for the past twenty-five years.

"Not a problem, Mia, and you are too sweet. Have a good day," he said to me as he turned and starting to walk back down toward the sidewalk.

"Have a good day," I told him as he was walking away.

"I think your company is coming," he said as a truck pulled into my driveway and the engine was turned off.

"Ms. Brown, Ms. Brown. I get to go to the park with you," Zoe announced very excited.

"Well good morning, Zoe, you sure are nice and chipper," I said bending down to give her a hug.

"Good morning Mia," Ben said as he approached my front door.

"Good morning," I replied. Noticing his outfit I commented, "You look like you just stepped out of a fitness magazine or something." He looked perfect: a sleeveless workout shirt, a pair of black shorts, and his immaculate tennis shoes that looked like they still belonged on the store shelf they were so clean. It was pretty obvious from the look of his arms that he worked out quite often and did care about his body, just looking at him made a shiver run down my spine.

He teased me, saying, "I have to look good while I am working out. Some pretty lady just might decide to want to take a walk with me and I have to be able to grab her attention."

"Can we go? Boots is getting too wild and I can hardly hold him any more," Zoe protested.

"Sure thing Toots," Ben replied with Zoe looking at him in frustration, obviously not liking the nickname her dad had chosen to call her.

We all walked down the sidewalk, Ben and I side by side and Zoe a few steps ahead going toward her bike. As Zoe climbed onto her bike Ben took the leash of the tiny maltese puppy that they had brought along for the walk. I reached out and rubbed a hand over the dog's soft, snow white fur. Ben explained that he had gotten the white pup just about two weeks before they learned of Laura's accident, and that Zoe had gotten really attached to it over the past few months.

I looked at Zoe riding her pink and white bike just a little ways in front of Ben and me. She was probably the sweetest child I'd ever taught. Her big, brown, puppy dog eyes and long brown hair made her almost irresistible. She had been so shy and quiet her first few weeks at school, and even then, just two weeks until the last day of school and she was still really quiet. She was always polite, saying "yes ma'am", "please" and "thank you." You could tell her father had high expectations of her when she was at home.

Ben and I chatted about nothing in particular on the way to the park. It was just nice strolling down the sidewalk beside him. It felt right somehow having him at my side and wondered if he felt the same way about me. There was a genuine bond that I felt between the two of us; an effortless relationship that just seemed to click at the restaurant last week.

We had walked around the entire park when Ben glanced down at me and asked, "Do you know what time it is?"

I looked at my cell phone that I was carrying in my pocket and answered, "It is four minutes after ten."

"Oh my gosh! I am supposed to have Zoe home, changed for practice, and there by ten thirty. It takes me fifteen minutes just to get her hair into a decent ponytail," he exclaimed looking to round up his daughter and head home.

"Hold on, Ben, I have an idea," I insisted.

Ben stopped and turned looking at me. He teased and asked, "What do you have a machine that stops time for a little while?"

"No, but it is actually better than that. I will give you some of my time," I said smiling. "I can take Zoe home with me, do her hair, give her a snack, and have her ready when you get back from your house with her practice clothes and pads," I offered and even threw in that I'd take the dog home with me and let him wander around my living room so Ben wouldn't be bothered with even that inconvenience.

"Wow, are you serious?" he asked me. "That would make it faster too, because you live closer to the park and soccer field so after I get her clothes on it'll be right there around the corner." He was very excited by then. "Sure, I'll let you if you are sure that it is okay with you," he accepted my offer.

"Zoe, come here honey. Dad has to go get your clothes for soccer practice, but sweet Mia here has offered for you and Mr. Boots to go home with her, she'll fix your hair, and I'll bring your things back there to change into," he explained, with Zoe getting more excited as the seconds went on.

"Yay, I get to go to Ms. Brown's house!" she said very excitedly.

Ben turned back around to face me with a look of gratitude all over his face. "Listen, I owe you on this one Mia. You have helped me abundantly and you have made her day," he said glancing at his daughter. He looked at his watch next saying, "I'll just be about 10 minutes, promise," he said and started off down the sidewalk to get his truck from my house.

I turned to look at Zoe waiting eagerly by with the white fluff ball of a dog. "Alright Zoe, it looks like it's just us two. Are you ready to go home with me?" I asked her, knowing the answer.

"Yes!" She answered and took my hand in her little one. We walked back down the sidewalk toward my house the whole time hand in hand while my heart was growing to love the little girl even more every minute that I was with her.

We stepped in the house, Zoe picking up the little white dog to bring him inside. I had her put him in the kitchen where he could get a drink and I came back with her into the living room. I grabbed a brush and ponytail holder out of the hall bathroom and sat down behind her. When I walked back into the living room Zoe was admiring all of the feminine touches spread throughout the house. Her bright eager eyes were looking all around as I approached the place where she was standing.

"How do you want me to fix your hair?" I asked Zoe, knowing that would be a rare treat getting her hair fixed.

"I want a braid, no, two braids please," she said reminding me that it was how her best friend at school, Bethany, always wore her hair.

I had her sit down on the floor in front of me and I began work on the two braids that she had requested so politely. Zoe asked question about my house, things I like to do, and other various things as I worked on her hair. She was so eager and excited to hear about shopping and other girl activities that I enjoyed doing.

Just as I was finishing up the last braid her father walked through the front door and looked at the two of us plopped down on the floor.

Zoe glowed with pride as she saw Ben walking across the living room floor. "Daddy, look what Mia did to my hair. I have two braids just like my friends," she exclaimed. Next she added quite honestly, "I like her even more at home than I do at school."

Laughing, I thanked Zoe for the compliment and grabbed her clothes from Ben, who, up until then had basically just stood and smiled at his daughter. I am sure

Ben could tell that Zoe who was obviously happier than she'd been in quite some time.

"Here, precious, let me help you with your shirt so we don't mess up those pretty braids in your hair, and then you can go to the bathroom and change your shorts," I told her as I slid her hot pink tank top over her head.

Zoe hugged me and ran off to the bathroom. I walked over to Ben, worried about his sudden quietness.

"Are you okay," I asked him, putting my hand on his back.

He turned around to look at me with a glistening tear on his lower eyelid. He smiled at me, settling my nerves just somewhat, and then spoke to me.

"Mia, I cried when Laura died, and I cried when we buried my grandfather when I was twenty one years old, but this is the first tear that I've ever had because of happiness," he admitted. Going on, he said, "I've never seen Zoe so happy in all of her six years on this earth. She's never had her hair in braids since her dad was all thumbs when it comes to fixing girls' hair. She actually has had a better time today than she's ever had. Thank you so much! But I have to admit it scares me," he said and again turned his back to me and looked out the window.

"What are you afraid of?" I asked quietly, walking up behind him, standing close enough that I could feel the electric spark between us.

"That Zoe and I will lose you, too. That you won't stick around and Zoe won't have enough of these types of days," he told me.

Reaching up to touch his shoulder, I gently turned him around to face me.

"Listen, Ben, this is all new for me. If I can be completely honest right now, I will tell you I've never been in a relationship that has meant anything to me. It's been one date here and there and then it's over. I am scared to death right now because I am having feelings I've never felt. Yes, it feels good and right somehow. But, life is a gamble; we never know how it'll play out. But, I can promise you I am willing to give us a try if you are willing to also," I ended my little confession.

He gently placed his hands on my shoulders and standing dangerously close, spoke in a low, husky voice. "Mia, there are things about my past, about my marriage to Laura that I'm not ready to talk about quite yet. However, I can tell you that I've never felt this way about another woman, nor had anyone been so motherly to my daughter as you have been. Thank you, and yes, I'd love to give us a shot," he answered me. He then leaned in close to my face and brushed a soft kiss on my cheeks just as Zoe entered the room.

I looked in her direction. "Well, look at you," I exclaimed. " You are a true little princess if I've ever seen one," I said lovingly. "Okay Zoe, you promise me that you will try your hardest at practice today and be extra good for your daddy. If you keep your end of the bargain then I'll promise to take you to the zoo right after school is out," I promised her.

"Yay," she squealed hugging me tightly. "Mia," she spoke more in more of a question than as if she were just saying my name.

"Yes, honey," I answered back.

"Do you like me and my daddy," she asked?

I looked at Ben, then back down at Zoe. Kneeling down and taking her little face in my hands I gave her a sweet kiss on her forehead and answered her, "Zoe sweetie, I have liked you since the first day you walked into my classroom at school and that isn't going to change. And yes, I do really like your daddy too. He makes me happy just like you do."

Zoe leaned over to give me a hug. "Mia, I love you," she spoke softly hugging my neck.

I had to clear my throat before I could speak another word. I wiped a tear from the corner of my eye before it escaped and fell to the floor. I looked at my watch realizing now what time it must be.

"Babe, you and your dad had better get to practice or you'll be late," I said to her.

"Ok, bye Mia," she waved as she headed toward the door.

Ben looked at me and mouthed the words "thank you," as he took his daughter's hand and walked off down the front sidewalk.

I closed the door and walked to my couch, throwing myself down on the cushiony pillows. I felt nervous, happy, and scared all at the same time. "What have I gotten myself into?" I asked Snowball as he curled up on my lap. Looking up to the ceiling I thanked God for placing both Zoe and Ben in my life. I then closed my eyes and drifted off to sleep. I had the most incredible dream about Ben and myself while I was asleep. I wore a long white wedding dress and he sported a black tuxedo. Zoe was wearing a crown of flowers on her head and was throwing petals on the floor of a huge church. When I awoke I was sad that the dream was over, though hopeful about today's events, and worried that, like the dream, this whole wonderful situation would disappear.

CHAPTER 13

Summer Is Finally Here!

The last couple of weeks of school flew by. I had my kindergarten graduation and was so proud of Zoe when she walked in wearing the blue graduation hat that we had made the day before in school. She had done really well about acting normal at school around me, even though ours was nowhere near a normal student/teacher relationship. Ben and I continued to see each other more and more. We would find ways to spend time with each other any way possible and lots of those times included Zoe in the plans. Some of our dates included me nervously cooking for Zoe and her father- the professional chef. Other things we did together was going to the movies to see the new cartoon out on film and going to the park for picnics and playtime.

Ben told me he was arranging some time for just the two of us once school was out. We had been seeing each other for about a month and most of the plans that we'd had were filled with other people around us. This night was to be for him and myself, time to talk and learn more about one another. Zoe was going to be spending two nights with her grandparents, Laura's mom and dad. Ben had asked me if I wanted to come over to his house for dinner on that Friday night, and that he was taking the evening off from work. I accepted the invitation nervously because I had been out with Ben longer than any other guy ever. He had been a complete gentleman the entire time. However, we would be alone at his house this time. I really like him, but I was praying that he would not push for a more intimate relationship that I was not willing to give into before marriage. I had held strong to my morals for years, and any man worth being with would accept that as a good thing and not push.

Ben only lived about two miles across town from me. Since it was such a beautiful night, I decided to walk to his house for supper. I walked up to the front door and saw a note stuck to the glass that read: Mia, come around to the back of the house. I followed the stepping-stones to the back of the house and saw a huge blanket with a basket and plates setting in the middle. Ben exited from his house through the French doors carrying a bottle of wine in one hand and towing wine glasses in the other.

"Good evening, Mia, you look stunning," he said as the gentle summer breeze floated through the hot air.

"Good evening yourself, but don't be silly. How can shorts and a polo be stunning?" I laughed, thinking it was sweet of him to call me stunning, no matter how untrue it was.

"Honey, you could wear your oldest and dirtiest clothes and still be beautiful to me. I get lost in your gorgeous ocean blue eyes and usually never even pay attention to what you are wearing anyway," he admitted. *If anyone's eyes were pretty enough to get lost in it would be his* I thought to myself as I looked into his dark brown almond eyes that looked back at me in loving admiration.

I walked over and gave him a soft hug and sat down on the over sized blue blanket that lay on the ground. I kicked my flip-flops off to the side to let my bare feet rest against the blanket he had laid out for us.

"Have a glass of wine and some cheese. I will be right back out. I just need to get one more thing inside," he told me.

I watched him disappear through the doors back into the house. He reappeared about two or three minutes later with his hands behind his back.

"What are you doing?" I laughed as he was trying to hide his secret behind his back very awkwardly.

He walked over and asked me to stand up, so I did.

He began to speak being very serious. "Mia, I have been happier in the past month than I can ever remember. Zoe has been a different child and we can both thank you for that. So, I want to give you something to show you how grateful I am for our relationship." He pulled a dozen red lilies out from behind his back with one of his hands and handed them to me.

"Oh my goodness, they are absolutely gorgeous," I began as I took them into my hands and smelled the sweet scent coming from them. "How did you know that these were one of my favorites?" I asked feeling the sweetness of his actions take over my senses.

"I have my ways," he winked. "But, I have one more thing to go with it." He pulled out his other hand, baring a single long stemmed white calla lily. "*Cara Mia*, this white calla lily stands out in beauty and grace from all the other red flowers that you are holding now. You, my darling, are just like this calla lily, standing out among all the other women that I have ever known. Let this be a symbol of your beauty and kindness and please give me the pleasure of saying you'll officially be my girlfriend," he ended his speech and handed the calla lily to me to add to the rest of the flowers.

A tear dropped from my blue eyes and rolled down my cheek, causing him to raise his fingers to my face and gently brush it away. I could hardly breathe, let alone try to speak. I cleared my throat and placed a gentle but loving kiss on his soft lips. "I would be honored to call myself your girlfriend, my darling," I somehow answered before tip toeing and wrapping my arms around his strong shoulders and neck. And for the second time since I had met Ben I felt like a young teenage girl falling for her first true love.

Ben pulled me away from him and asked me to come sit on the blanket with him. He said he had something very important to talk to me about before our relationship went any further.

"Mia, I want you to understand why it is so easy to fall in love with you so soon after Laura's death," he continued obviously wanting me to hear the whole truth about him and Laura.

He began to speak in an honest and soft-spoken voice. "When Laura and I were dating we had a really different relationship. Our views on children, religion, politics, and every other important topic were completely different. I think I knew before her that we weren't in love with each other. However, it was familiar and easy so I continued to date her. Laura was somewhat of a needy woman, she constantly wanted something, and being very determined, she usually got what she was after. The summer my mom and dad returned from mission work in Africa they were so sick that they were barely surviving. I was a total mess and the only one there to take care of them. I was physically and emotionally run down. That same summer, Laura decided that with me so vulnerable and her ready to have a very intimate relationship, that she was ready for us to give ourselves to each other entirely, hoping that I would cave on my principals of waiting until marriage. She knew my feelings, but being selfish and willing to push for what she wanted, she continued her hunt," he stopped and looked at me to see what my reactions were.

I just scooted a little closer, seeing how uncomfortable this was for him and urged him to keep going.

"Well, Laura asked me to come to her apartment one night after I'd had a really hard time with Mom and Dad. Anyway, Laura got what she wanted and more. What we hadn't bargained on was that nine months later we would be welcoming little Zoe into the world. She was the most precious little miracle I'd ever seen and immediately fell in love with her. I wasn't so much in love with Laura, but felt that it would be the right thing to do if I asked her to marry me. You know the rest. I never really felt for her what a normal married man would for his wife, but felt it was necessary for our daughter. Of course, her being absent from the relationship so much just let the ties loosen even that much more before the accident ever even occurred. I've never before felt the feelings that I have for you, Mia," he said sweetly, smiling affectionately, while looking deep into my eyes.

He continued, "Laura never wanted to be a mom, not that early in her life, anyway. She wanted excitement and adventure. That's why she joined the armed forces, which I looked up to her for doing. But then, when she came home and took up a life that kept her on the run working for the government, I realized she was never going to be the domestic wife that I so wanted to have. I had to face the fact that I wouldn't come home from work to see her holding our daughter in her arms and giving me a kiss to welcome me home," he finished.

"So, you basically raised Zoe all by yourself then," I said. "Weren't you ever bitter toward Laura?" I asked.

"Yes, and no," he answered and went on to explain. "Laura stayed around for the most part for the first few months. Then she got bored, which is when she decided she'd serve her country, which had been her plans before she got pregnant anyway. I have a real admiration for the men and woman in the service and I think she knew that. She felt like that this would make it okay for her to be gone so much."

"Wow, this really does answer a lot of my questions. Not that I questioned how you could feel for me the way you do so shortly after Laura's..." I didn't have time to finish before Ben was butting in.

"Yeah, you never wondered but yet you are talking about it," he said smiling.

"Ok, maybe I wondered a little, but I always try to tell myself that without the whole story I can't pass judgment. I have learned that from teaching kids. In order to fully understand a story you have to have all sides," I said.

"You probably think that I am silly and old-fashioned to want to wait until marriage to give myself to a woman, don't you?" he asked me shyly.

"On the contrary Ben, I have had the same expectations since I was a little girl. I grew up in a very strict and religious home and still to this day I've stuck to those same morals and principals. I thank God all the time for the parents He blessed me with and the faith they brought me up with.

Sometimes I look at others who don't believe, or who were not brought up with the faith of God and wonder how they cope with the trials and heartaches of life," I admitted. "I have a lot more to be thankful for now than ever before."

"Well, I think we've gotten everything out in the open and we can now date each other with no secrets and knowing exactly what we each expect out of the relationship," he stated on a livelier note.

"I might need some pointers, I'm not really good at the dating thing. I've had relationships that last, uh let's see, one date," I laughed, while still being completely serious.

"Well, I'm not the most experienced either," he said laughing too. "We really are a great pair, huh?" he said, knowing that indeed we were good for each other and I was good for Zoe as well, which made me feel really good.

We finished a magnificent dinner In Ben's backyard. The conversation drifted to much lighter topics such as: favorite foods, sports, and hobbies that we are both into. The evening was wonderful, romantic, everything I could have dreamt it would be. Ben knew how to make a woman feel important and special; he was the kind of man I'd been waiting to meet all of my life.

When I got up to leave Ben offered to drive me home. I accepted his invitation and climbed into his car. I didn't let him take me because I was tired and it wasn't because it was getting dark, I simply didn't want the date to end.

He drove the two and a half miles across town to my house without saying much at all. Our hands were clasped and we listened to the music that played on his radio. He pulled into my drive and turned the keys in the ignition off.

We looked at each other and started to talk at the same time.

"I," we said in unison.

"Go ahead Mia, ladies first," he gestured.

"I was just going to say that I had a great evening with you and I'm glad you felt like you could talk to me about your past," I told him.

"Me too," he said. "I think you might have a spell on me. I feel like I can always tell you anything, even about some things that I have never told anyone," he added.

I waved my finger around mysteriously as if holding a magic wand, "You never know what kind of magic I have up my sleeves," I teased.

"Oh, I'll have to watch it from now on then. If I misbehave you might turn me into frog or something," he joked.

"I would never turn you into a frog, at least not on purpose," I said laughing. "Well, I'll see you soon I hope," I told him as I reached for the door handle so that I could climb out and go into my empty house.

Ben gently grabbed my free hand and pulled me to him stopping me about an inch from his face. "Darling, you might just get tired of me if I see you as much as I'd like to," he breathed out heavily, looking straight into my eyes.

My legs were now like Jell-o and I couldn't think or see clearly. I wanted him to kiss me so badly yet the anticipation of the kiss itself was exhilarating.

At that very minute he closed the one-inch gap that had separated us, and gently placed a kiss on my lips that would last until the next time I saw him. We separated and he gently slid his thumb over my lips. Then, pulling back, he blew me a kiss goodnight and I stepped out into the now dark sky. He waited until I was in my house before driving away and I stood at the door watching the taillights of his truck disappear around the bend.

When I got inside I knew that there was no hope of me getting to sleep anytime soon. Thoughts of Ben were twirling around my mind. I changed my clothes and got into bed reaching to my bedside to grab a book to read. My mind was floating to and from the book making it impossible to keep straight what was going on in the story. I decided to turn on the TV and watch the bedtime news before I turned out the lights and made myself try to get some sleep. Just as I was about to turn the lights out my cell phone started to buzz on the night stand, letting me know I had a text message. When I lifted the flap to my phone I saw three words that melted my heart and told me that sleep was definitely something that was not coming soon or easy. Ben had texted three little words that mean more than any other three words I could think of. Looking at the screen I read, "I LOVE YOU!!"

CHAPTER 14

The Horrible End to a Perfect Night

The next six months flew by. Ben and I spent lots of time together and included Zoe in most things that we did. Over summer break we took her to the zoo, swimming, and even took her to the mountains to stay in a cabin about four hours from Springsville, where both of our houses were. Zoe and I shared a room on that trip and Ben roomed with Boots. We had a wonderful time, it being the first trip that Zoe had ever been on. She was filled with amazement and wonder at the sight of the mountains, shops, and all of the people.

Ben, Zoe, and I grew closer and closer over the summer and into the Fall. I had gotten to where I felt like her mother, which was no longer awkward since I wasn't her teacher anymore. She would come to my classroom after school everyday and I would drive her home to the babysitter, or even sometimes take her to my house until her dad got off work. She was thrilled at this because it meant she didn't have to ride the hot, stinky school bus, as she called it. I could tell it was really good for Zoe having a female in her life, she seemed happier than I think I had even seen her over the last year and few months that I'd known her.

LeAnne and my mother were the most thrilled for me about my relationship with Ben. LeAnne couldn't stop telling me what a hottie I'd gotten. I knew that what she was saying was absolutely true. However, it was what was on the inside that really made me fall in love with him. I can remember telling LeAnne over lunch one day that he was the most thoughtful and romantic man I'd ever known. It made me feel good that my best friend accepted him and was happy about our relationship.

My mom was another story in itself. From the day that I told her I had a boyfriend she was on me every day wanting to know how things were going, was he treating me well, was I being nice to him, etcetera. I felt like she was a drill sergeant calling me everyday for a relationship update. I didn't mind too awful much, though, because I knew it was just because she cared and wanted me happy. Of course, she commented that she would love to have more grandchildren, too.

It was then just two weeks until Christmas and I had just about finished my shopping. Ben had invited me to come to a Christmas party at the Stone Hallow Inn. I took a quick shower after work that day and pulled on some black pants and a red sweater suitable for a Christmas party, and headed out the door.

The winter air was cold against my bare face and hands. I climbed into my car and headed toward the restaurant with the heat blasting. There was a small amount of snow that had not melted and gathered at the edge of the road. I drove slowly to the restaurant that I wouldn't hit a slick spot and lose control of my car. On my way from my house to the restaurant I saw three vehicles off the side of the road so I knew it was still slick.

My cell phone started to play my favorite classical piece, "Cannon in D", alerting me that Ben was calling me.

"Hello," I answered.

"Hey, honey, where are you?" he asked in a concerned voice.

"I'm just about two miles away, the roads are slick and I'm having to drive pretty slowly," I told him.

"I was starting to get a little worried. I've heard that there have been a lot of accidents on the roads today," he said to me.

"I should be there in just a few minutes," I promised him, easing his mind. "And I will be extra careful, I promise."

"Love you, *Cara Mia*, till the stars go away," he said to me, just like he always said to his daughter, making me feel extra special and loved.

"Love you till the sun stops shining," I told him, making up my own ending for the perfectly sweet conclusion to a conversation.

I put my phone down in the seat next to me and worked on driving the last two miles very carefully. About five minutes later, I pulled into the restaurant parking lot, parked the car, and struggled through the cold wind to get inside.

"Ah, *Cara Mia*, I am so glad you are here," Ben greeted me with a big bear hug to try and warm me up. He guided me over to where the fireplace was burning and let me feel the comfort of the heat coming from it. I smelled the aroma of cinnamon and pine needles from the enormous Christmas tree mingling throughout the air.

"I hope you are hungry, I have more appetizers than I know what to do with," he bragged.

"Well then, it's a good thing your whole staff is here to help us eat it all then. And yes, I am starved," I told him as we started toward the table.

Seeing all of his staff arranged around the long rectangular table I felt a twinge of pride in Ben. He was so thoughtful and generous with his staff.

"Ben, I think it is great that you throw a Christmas party for your staff here each year," I admitted to him.

"It's the least I can do for the people that help get me and this business through the year," he said in response to my compliment.

I walked along, looking at the beautiful Christmas decorations. There were two big trees trimmed in silver and gold. Large green garland with lights draped across each of the massive doorways.

"You did a wonderful job decorating this place Ben," I said teasingly, knowing that he'd hired someone to come in and decorate it for him.

"Why thank ya, ma'am," he said in a strong Southern accent and then laughed at himself.

"Hey, Mia," Zoe came running up to me, giving me a huge hug.

"Hi, Honey," I said back. Looking at Ben I commented, "I'm glad your dad let you come this year."

Ben smiled and replied, "Yes, but there's a good reason for her to be here this year," he said, knowing I would know he meant to be with me.

I smiled in return and took Zoe's hand, following her daddy toward a table to set down. Ben led us to the long table in the middle of the restaurant with Christmas centerpieces lining the table. There were already many seats filled when we came up to it.

"Hi Mia, you sure had this fool worried sick about you," Bo teased, patting Ben on the back. "Glad to see you again" he said, smiling at me.

"You too, Bo," I answered back. The last time I'd seen Bo was when he, his wife, Ben, and I had gone bowling together. He and his wife had beat Ben and I so bad.

"Hi," I said to his wife, who was sitting next to him.

"Hey Mia, glad you made it okay. The roads are just horrible out there," she said back to me.

Everyone else took their turns in greeting me at the table and I, in return, said hi to them. I didn't really know anybody enough to carry on a conversation, but that was why I was glad Zoe was there with me. I knew I'd be able to talk to her and keep busy by helping her with her plate. I was hoping no one would notice that I seemed to be a little shy and timid around everyone that was there.

Ben started the dinner off with a speech to his staff about what a wonderful year they had made it for him, helping out when things were rough for him. He told them that he hoped the upcoming year would be just as successful as well. Looking at me and winking he admitted that he hoped for big things to happen in his business and I his personal life, leaving everyone to whistle and raise their glasses for a toast. We all stood to go to the buffet line, Zoe sticking to my side.

"This is unbelievable," I said looking at all the food in front of us. There were dips, cheese balls, meatballs, cocktail shrimp, salads, and more. "Even the presentation is amazing," I complimented Ben.

"Thank you, my lady," he said. "I do try to please."

We all filled our plates and returned to our seats to enjoy the food that had been prepared. The meal was absolutely fabulous and the company even better than the food. Everybody was so nice, and having Zoe and Ben on either side of me was nice and cozy feeling.

When I finished eating and visiting with all of the remarkably nice people that worked for Ben, I went to tell him that I needed to go because I had to get up early the next morning to go shopping. I had to finish up some last minute Christmas shopping for Zoe and her daddy.

I hugged Zoe goodnight and gave her a sweet kiss on the cheeks. "I could take Zoe home if you want me to," I said looking at Ben.

"No, no. She can stick around a little while longer. You need to get your sleep and she needs to help her daddy a little after everyone is gone," he assured me. "But thank you very much for the offer."

Ben excused himself from the table to walk me out. I told everyone goodbye and Merry Christmas before following Ben to the front door.

"Mia, please be careful, it's starting to snow again. Would you like for me to take you home?" he asked me.

"No, I'll go slow and be fine, promise. It is very sweet of you to worry about me, though. I haven't had the pleasure of having someone worry about me since my mom and dad moved to Florida," I told him.

"I love you so much, *Cara Mia*," Ben stated lovingly while helping me put my winter coat on so that I wouldn't freeze out there. After my coat was on he wrapped me in his arms and looked lovingly into my eyes.

Ben had been calling me *Cara Mia*, instead of just Mia for a while now. I had noticed it, but never really thought that much about it. About two weeks before, I found out that when Ben called me *Cara Mia*, it meant My Darling in Italian. Ever since then I had gotten cold chills every time he used his Italian accent call me that.

"I love you too my darling," I said in return, using the English version for my response.

He kissed me on the forehead before giving me a passionate kiss that caused my legs to feel weak and my breathing to speed up. Finally, letting go a couple of minutes later, he told me to be careful again and warned me to call him when I got home so that he could be sure I was fine.

"Yes sir," I responded, as if he were my father giving me orders. I turned my head and headed out into the worsening storm. The snow was picking up now and the roads were practically covered again.

I got in the car and started the engine, letting it run a few minutes before I started off so it could warm up some. I exited the parking lot and turned left to head home. I flipped on the radio to hear Christmas music fill my vehicle, which finished the evening off nicely. Going through town I admired the illuminated and snow covered streets. The light ahead at the intersection remained green so I continued to drive with out having to use my brakes. Out of the corner of my eyes I noticed a green car coming from the left going much faster than I felt it should be on these slick roads, since they were going to have to be stopping at the red light.

When I was directly under the red light my body froze with fear as I saw the car running through it and coming straight at me. I felt as if everything were going in slow motion as I let out an ear splitting scream, braced myself, and then felt the impact of the other car crashing into my side.

All I could feel was pain all over my body. I could smell gasoline in the air and feel the cold snow coming through the shattered windows and landing on my burning face. Next, the pain in my body started to ease as every inch of me started to become numb and, slowly, my eyes started to close. All I could think about as I started to drift off was Ben and Zoe, who were at the restaurant cleaning up from the Christmas party that had just ended.

CHAPTER 15

My Worst Nightmare

I don't know what is going on but I just have a horrible feeling that something was wrong. I cleared the last plate off the table and felt a strange sensation in the pit of my stomach.

"Zoe, are you okay honey," I hollered out through the empty restaurant, making sure that she was fine.

"I'm right here, Dad," Zoe yelled from the kitchen where she was cleaning off the counters for me. Just then, I heard sirens screaming by the restaurant, outside in the bitter winter storm. I always worried about the person that the ambulance was going to get every time I heard a siren in town. I took a second to say a prayer for whomever they were going to get.

Continuing to clean the table, I shook my head and tried to lay the feeling to rest, knowing it must just be all the food I ate making me feel sick. I went to look for Bo, who had stayed around to help me clean up before taking his wife home. They were going to go home and trim their Christmas tree, but he said he had a half hour or so that he could help to clean up. *I don't know what I would do around here sometimes without my best friend* I thought.

The phone in the kitchen rang and I asked Zoe if she would get it. Bo must have been in there though because I heard a male voice answering the phone. It was probably another late caller wanting to reserve a Christmas party date at the restaurant. I had been bombarded the past week with reservations for parties and family gatherings. It was getting a little late for that now, however. Most of the dates had already been reserved.

A couple of minutes later, Bo came out of the kitchen looking horrified.

"What's wrong Bo? You look like you have seen a ghost," I said to him, a little nervous from the look he was giving me.

"Uh, Ben, sit down, big guy," Bo commanded me very sternly.

"What is it man? You are scaring me," I told him, refusing to sit down like he had said. My mind immediately flashed to my mom and dad who were both in very bad shape. "Is it Mom or Dad?" I questioned him, wanting to know which it was.

"No Ben, there's been an accident, a wreck in town," he stammered. "It's, it's…" he muttered, unable to get out the words that he was trying to find.

"Damn it Bo, come on, who is it? Come on and tell me man. You're scaring me," I said again, urging him to tell me knowing in the pit of my stomach that I really didn't want to hear who it was.

"Ben, it was Mia," was all he could say, and immediately I fell to my knees as the feeling in my legs and feet went away. I knew from the look on Bo's face that it wasn't good, and I didn't think I could handle this again. I had lost my wife a year and a half before. I didn't think I could handle losing the love of my life.

Bo pulled me to my feet and told me we needed to get to the hospital as quick as possible. He practically dragged me to his car, telling me that his wife would take home Zoe with her in his truck, and not to worry about her.

We pulled out onto the deserted road and my mind was reeling with thoughts and fear as to what I would find when I got to the hospital.

Chapter 16

Cara Mia, Please Don't Go

Bo drove me to the hospital where Mia was taken. I quickly took the elevator, cursing it for taking so long to reach the floor where the trauma unit was housed. I stepped off, looking frantically in both directions for a desk to ask where I could find Mia. The whole time I had been hoping and praying that I would walk in and she would be setting up just fine, waiting for me to get her. I knew down deep though that if they sent her to the trauma unit that I wasn't going to be so lucky.

I finally found a desk where a young nurse was on the computer and quickly walked up to it.

"Excuse me ma'am, I am Ben Allegra, Mia Brown's boyfriend. Can you tell me anything about her or where I can see her?" I asked in a very scared voice.

"Sir, the doctors are in with her now. You won't be able to see her yet. I don't know anything for sure, but I do know that she was pretty messed up. You may want to go ahead and prepare yourself for the worst," she said sadly as I began to melt right there in the hall.

The nurse came back over and put her hand on my shoulder, " I promise I will let you know something as soon as I hear, or when the doctor's come out," she promised me. "Now, why don't you go sit down in the waiting room while you wait for some news," she urged me. "I am sure they will have to run a battery of tests on her."

After thanking the nurse, I started to pace around the waiting room. Every minute that passed was like torture, taking forever and ever.

Finally, a man wearing a long white coat, surgical gloves, and a mask came walking out of from the back. He walked over to the nurses' station and put some information into the computer before the nice nurse that I had been talking to started discussing something with him and pointing in my direction. I looked at him anxiously as he walked in my direction with a very serious look on his face.

He reached out his hand to introduce himself. "Hello, I'm Dr. Taylor. I've been working with Mia since she got here," he stated.

"How is she? Can I see her? Is she going to make it?" I asked all of these questions very quickly.

"Ben, I don't want to lie to you; she is not in good shape. According to a witness, an elderly driver slid through the red light just as Mia was going through and hit her on the driver's side door. When the EMS arrived on the scene she was unconscious, and she is in a coma now. She had a broken leg, collarbone, and crushed left wrist. We won't know if there is any permanent damage until she wakes up and the next twenty-four hours will be crucial to answering the question "if" she will wake up. I am sorry, I wish I had better news to tell you sir," he finished.

"Oh my sweet Jesus, let her be okay," I begged of God, looking up toward Heaven. I really didn't know what I would do without her in my life. And Zoe, she had become the mother that Zoe never knew.

The doctor continued by saying, "You can go in, but she is on life support at this time helping her to breath, and there are lots of cords hooked up to her. She is already bruising in her face and has some swelling. I just want you to be prepared to see her how she is," he said flatly. "Who knows, though, sometimes when a patient hears a loved one's voice it will help to bring them out of the coma, or at least help them have a reason to fight. You have fifteen minutes with her. Be positive and don't sound upset. Remember that even though she is in a coma she may very well be able to hear you," he instructed me.

I followed Dr. Taylor through the doors and into room 221, Mia's room. I walked into the dimly lit room hearing the sound of machines beeping and of oxygen being pumped into Mia's fragile body. I looked at the bed and saw a lifeless, delicate flower lying under the sheets. I walked to her bedside, and tears started to flow down my cheeks. Her beautiful hair was covered with a white bandage and her arm was in a brace, lying gently by her side.

I walked up beside her bed, sat down, and very gently took her hand in mine. It lay in my hand, cold and unmoving. I bent my head, and lay on her bedside, and wept quietly.

"Oh Mia, why did this have to happen? I should have taken you home. I shouldn't have let you go," I told her, hating myself at that point for not demanding that I drive her home.

I looked at her swollen and bruised face through tear-filled eyes and begged her to be strong and come back to Zoe and me.

"We need you, Mia. You've been more of a mom to Zoe than she's ever had and I've never loved a woman like I love you. Don't leave us. Please God let her stay, don't take her from me," I begged.

One of the machines at her bedside started beeping violently and two doctors rushed in and forced me into the hall.

"What's going on?" I screamed through the closing door. "Is it something I said, is she going to be okay?" I asked, scared to death at what might happen.

A nurse hurried by me and went into the room, closing the door completely, and leaving me alone in the quiet hallway. I stood there not moving, hoping for the best but fearing the worst. *Did I do something, did she hear me crying, and is this the end for my sweet Mia*? I thought to myself in fear.

Chapter 17

Where Am I?

"Why is everything so white?" I said aloud. *Everything is so quiet and peaceful; I can't feel the pain anymore.*

"Where am I?" I asked, hoping someone would listen to me and have an answer. I saw a shadow, a figure coming toward me.

"Mia," the figure whispered.

"Who are you, and where am I?" I wanted to know, asking who I saw to be a beautiful lady dressed in white.

"I am Laura, Ben's late wife," the lady answered.

"But you are...does that mean that I am...," I couldn't get out what I was wanting to ask her. I thought to myself that I must be in Heaven, it was so peaceful and everything looked so soft and white.

"No, Mia, you are not dead. You are asleep and have been hurt very badly," she said to me.

"But, why can't I feel anything? Am I going to die? Have you come to take me to Heaven?" I asked her. I wasn't quite afraid, but was not ready to leave the life that I still had so much of to live.

"No, Mia, I have come to tell you to fight. You have to go back and heal. You have a wonderful mission that God has chosen me to tell you about. You are to go back and marry Ben. You have to take care of him and raise my darling little Zoe like she were your own child. Do you understand God's plan for you?" she asked me.

"Yes, but. . ." I started, but was cut off in mid-sentence.

"There are no but's Mia, God has chosen you to raise this child, His child," she stated. "Now, go back. Back to Ben and help his life with that beautiful little girl be complete. He will need you Mia. Go, fight to heal and get strong," she instructed.

Just as I began to say something else, Laura started to drift away, getting smaller and smaller until she became but a piece of dust in the distance and then she was gone.

All of the sudden I started to feel a stinging sensation in my legs. It spread throughout my whole body. I felt like my head was going to explode. Next, I heard beeping noises and strange distant voices hurrying around me. I began to feel afraid now; I couldn't open my eyes. Why couldn't I move my legs? What was happening to me?

One of the voices said, "Her heart rate is coming back down, she is stabilizing again. What got her so excited?" I heard the voices asking.

"I don't know, but her vitals are getting even better," the other voice answered back.

There was more movement, and then I heard a door open and close.

"You can come in now, everything is okay," one of the voices was telling someone.

"Oh my gosh, what happened?" the voice asked. "Did I say something or do something to upset her?" the new, yet familiar voice asked.

I felt a warm hand grasp my burning hand.

"Mia, my darling, I wish I knew if you could hear me," the familiar voice, I figured out was Ben. I tried to move, to open my eyes, but I couldn't. I felt like a turtle stuck inside of its shell, unable to come out.

Feeling Ben rub my cheek ever so gently, I started to feel sleepy and before I knew it, I was fast asleep.

CHAPTER 18

Finally, There's Hope

"Hey there, Ben, how's she doing?" Mia's mom asked as she entered the waiting room Sunday morning. It had been over a week since Mia's accident and she was still in a coma. Other than to spend some time with Zoe, I hadn't left her side.

"No change, Rose," I answered her, sounding frustrated. She seemed to be getting stronger, her vitals better every day, but she still was not waking up.

"Who's been taking care of your restaurant dear," she asked concerned and knowing I hadn't been to work since the accident.

"My best friend, Bo, has been keeping things going for me. We keep in touch by cell phone, texting, and so on," I told her.

"Where is Bill?" I asked her speaking of her husband, Mia's dad. I really hit it off with Bill, and got along with him really great from the time they stepped off the plane and I picked them up to bring them to the hospital.

"He's down getting some coffee," she answered back. "He can't get his day started without his caffeine, you know," she reminded me.

"Ah yes, I do know how it is to be a coffee addict," I laughed finally being able to loosen up a bit since the doctors thought Mia was going to come out of the coma eventually.

"I would like to talk to you two together when he gets up here if you don't mind," I told her.

"Sure thing, honey," she answered me. I could tell Rose liked me also. She was always checking on me, asking if I needed anything. You can just tell when your girlfriend's family likes you, and that is what was making what I was about to do so much easier.

A few minutes passed by, and then I saw the elevator doors open and Bill got off. I saw Rose talking to him, and then they both headed over in my direction.

"Okay dear, what did you want to speak to Bill and me about?" she asked me.

"Well, you know Mia and I have been dating for quite a few months now. I have really grown close to her and love her deeply," I stopped for a second as tears started to form in my eyes.

"She loves you too, Ben, I can tell by the way she talks about you," she said.

"While she's been in here I've started to realize I don't want to live without her. So, if, no when, she wakes up I would like your blessing for me to ask her to marry me," I finally got out. I felt as if a ton of bricks had been lifted off my shoulders since I had finally gotten to ask her parents this question that had been on my mind for a few weeks.

Rose broke into tears, which really worried me making me, wonder if I'd done this too soon for her. Did she think I was moving too fast?

"I'm sorry, maybe it's too soon," I spoke apologetically.

"Oh no, no, no, my dear. I've dreamt of this moment since Mia met you. I could tell that you made her so happy and I also knew that you were a great guy. And who couldn't love little Zoe? I am just crying because, here we are, at the moment I have been waiting for, and Mia is not even conscious for it," she began to cry some more and gave me a big hug.

Bill spoke next, "My boy, I pray like crazy you get the chance to ask her that question real soon," he said, shaking my hand. "You have my blessings a thousand times over son."

I hugged them both and went back into Mia's room. She looked the same, although the bruises were starting to fade some, and the swelling in her beautiful face had basically all gone down.

I sat down beside her bed and took her delicate hand in mine just as I'd done many times in the past few days.

I laid my head over on the bed and said some prayers to God to bring her back to me, to us. As I was lying there I felt something move in my hand. I looked down to see a miracle: Mia's hand gently trying to squeeze mine.

"Oh my gosh, *Cara Mia*, can you hear me?" I asked overwhelmed with a sense of hope and joy at this point.

I saw her gently shake her head yes and I quickly leaned forward and kissed her on the cheek. "Oh baby, I love you. I have been so worried about you," I said as I pressed the nurse call button on her bedside.

The blonde nurse that I had come to know so well came through the door. "Do you need something, Mr. Allegra?" she asked.

"She's trying to squeeze my hand! I asked if she could hear me and she tried to shake her head yes!" I said very excitedly.

"Thank you for getting me Ben. Let me go get the doctor," she said, smiling. "I'll also tell her parents too, they are waiting out in the hall," she added as she was walking out the door.

"Thank you Nurse Browning," I said, smiling very hopefully and turning back to look at Mia.

"Oh, thank you, God. Thank you for bringing my Mia back to me," I spoke aloud very gratefully.

Rose burst through the doors first, quickly followed by Bill.

"Oh, my baby," she said looking at Mia first, and then me. "Is she waking up?" she questioned me.

"I don't know," I said but did tell her about Mia squeezing my hand.

I noticed Bill wipe a tear away from his eyes. He was more of the strong silent type, but Mia could pull some responses from him that no one else could.

"Excuse me, I hate to break up this party. I know you are all very excited, but I have to do some tests, exam Ms. Mia, to see if we can tell if there is going to be any long term damage," the doctor told us.

Rose, Bill, and I all stepped out into the hallway to give the doctor some time. The five minutes he was in with Mia seemed like an eternity, while I was in the hall waiting to see if her beautiful eyes were opened yet. When Dr. Taylor came into the hall he had a smile on his face.

"Well, I am cautiously optimistic about Mia's recovery. She is responding to all of my tests, but I need to send her down for more extensive testing. Also, with that hard bump on the head, we can't tell yet if there will be any long term effects until we get in and do a CAT scan. Things are definitely looking better now than even a half hour ago, though. I think Mia is finally on the right path," he reassured us.

"Okay, thanks, Dr. Taylor," Rose responded joyfully.

The three of us walked back into her room to tell her how much we loved her and to keep fighting. We weren't in there too long before two nurses came in and wheeled away Mia's bed with all of the cords so she could get the tests the doctor had ordered.

"I wish that when she comes back she would be awake," I whispered to myself.

Rose overheard my comment and came over to where I was standing. She put her arm around my shoulders. "Ben, we are all hoping for that, Honey. Let's go to the hospital chapel and say some prayers of Thanksgiving and some that her tests will all come out wonderfully," she said.

"Alright, that sounds great. God has brought her back this far. He will continue to help her, I am sure," I spoke, having faith in our Heavenly Creator.

We walked back to the familiar little chapel that we had spent so much time in praying for Mia's recovery. This time we came in Thanksgiving for what looked like was going to be a hopefully, full recovery.

When we walked in there were candles that gracefully lit the tiny room and flowers were placed at the front of the room; it was a perfect place to reflect and pray. It was a place to escape the struggles being fought within the hospital rooms.

We knelt down and made the sign of the cross before we began to say our prayers. I had been kneeling for what seemed like quite a while, so I glanced at the clock on the wall to check the time. I couldn't believe it when I saw that Mia had already been gone for an hour for her testing. They had told me the test would probably take a little less than an hour. I wondered if she was back in the room yet, and if she was awake and doing okay? It is funny how sometimes an hour seems like an eternity, and other times it flies by.

I looked at the large brown cross that hung on the wall and though about the fact that God loved us each so very much that He gave up His only son for us. Maybe today, He would have mercy on Mia and allow her to make a full recovery.

We looked around at each other as if we were thinking the same thing. I stood and was followed by both Rose and Bill. We left the little chapel and started back to Mia's room, none of us wanted to talk and break the peaceful silence we had found in that little room. We were all thinking about that princess lying in that bed fighting to return to us. Remembering her helpless and hurt body laying there, I again felt tears coming into my eyes.

As I rounded the corner to head back to the ICU/Trauma unit I saw a bed being wheeled down the hall. My hopes high that it was Mia, I quickly walked toward the two nurses who were guiding the bed along the white halls. Seeing what I had hoped for, Mia lying peacefully in the bed, I looked at her delicate body and my heart swelled with love for her. I had the sudden urge to wrap my arms around her and feel her arms around me.

They took her on into her room and told us the doctor would let us know the results as soon as he had them. Of course, it seemed as if we were waiting forever to hear back from the tests. Finally, the doctor walked into Mia's room with a hopeful smile on his face.

"Well, Doc, what did you find out about my little Mia?" Bill blurted out before the doctor could even close the door completely.

"Mr. Brown, I think you'll be pleased at what we found out with the tests," he said.

I couldn't help for my hopes to start to soar through the roof overhead as I eagerly waited for what the doctor was going to say.

Dr. Taylor started filling us in on what he had found out.

"We did a number of tests on Mia, and none of them indicated any signs of brain damage or anything else that could cause any long term effects," he stated. "The reason she is still asleep is her body is still using all of its energy to heal itself and her mind is keeping her asleep until she gets a little bit better."

"When will she wake up?" I asked, anxious to get to talk to my sweet girl.

"We can't tell exactly. However, the swelling on her brain has almost completely gone down, so we don't think it will be too much longer, but that is only speculation," he said. "I have to tell you I have seen cases where a patient has lain for a good month before their mind allowed them to wake up. I don't think that will be the case here, but I have to let you know all the possibilities," he told us. "What will be better than anything is for you all to continue to talk to her, hold her hand, and just be here. She will know you are here and might even be able to let you know she hears you at times," he told us.

"Being here and talking to her, now that is something I can definitely handle," I assured the doctor.

I sat down on the stool beside Mia's bed and looked down at her. All that I could think about was how beautiful she was and how I loved her and needed her more than anything else I could ever remember.

"*Cara Mia*, my darling. Won't you come back to me now? It just isn't the same without your smiling face and caring touch around here. Zoe has practically been living with sitters so that I can be here with you. She has been really patient, but she is ready for you to be better so you can come home and she can be with you and me again," I talked to Mia softly. "I want to take you home so we can be a family Mia. I love you," I told her and gently squeezed her soft hand.

At that very moment the miracle I had been waiting many days for came true. God himself gave me the best Christmas present I could ever get. Mia opened her beautiful eyes and smiled a gentle smile at me. Tears filled my eyes as Bill, Rose, and I all hugged our sweet girl and welcomed her back to us.

Chapter 19

Finally Home

As I opened my weak eyes I saw on of the best sights I could have hoped for; Ben was standing over me smiling that sweet smile.

"Mia, baby, it is so good to see those beautiful eyes of yours," Ben said to me. "How do you feel?"

I opened my mouth and tried to talk, but what came out was very frail.

"Ben, what happened? I don't remember a thing," I answered him.

"Honey, you were in a car accident the night you left the Christmas party at the restaurant. You have been here in a coma for almost two weeks," Ben told me. He went on to explain about the older man who had run into me and about how much I had been through since then.

"Oh my, you are kidding. I don't remember any of that. Is the man that hit me ok? Was anyone with him?" I asked concerned.

"My sweet Mia. Here you are just out of a coma and you are thinking about other people," Ben said to me. "He is okay and he was by himself. He broke his arm and was treated and released the night of the accident. He has been here a couple of times to check in on you and feels horrible for what happened. We told him we don't blame him for a thing. It was very slick that night and his car skidded into yours on the slippery ice," he explained.

"We, who is we?" I asked Ben.

Just then my mom and dad both walked from the corner of the room and gave me a gentle kiss.

"Mom, Dad, how long have you been here?" I asked them.

"Mia, we came the night that the accident happened. We have stayed here with you and have gone to your house once a day to take care of Snowball for you. You don't think we would stay in Florida with you in a coma do you?" they asked me as I held on to both of their hands.

Ben spoke up next. "You know Mia, I have been here almost the whole time and the same thing has been going through my mind each and every minute I sat and watched you, praying for your recovery," he said.

"What's that?" I questioned him, wondering what he might say.

"That I realize I don't want to live without you and that you mean more to me than almost anyone in this world," he stated honestly as he leaned over and gave me a kiss on the cheek.

Before I could comment on what Ben had just said a nurse walked into the room.

"Ben, did you buzz..." she started to say but stopped when she saw me with my eyes open, looking up at her.

"Mia, when did you wake up?" she asked me smiling.

"Just a few minutes ago," I answered weakly.

"Well, let's get the doctor back in here to check on you, okay," she said, and walked back out of the room. The elderly nurse patted my dad's back as she exited through the big door.

The doctor that came into my room was super sweet. He had been there the night that I was brought in after my wreck and had done everything possible to ensure that I made it. I owed him so much.

After getting a complete check up from the doctor I was told that everything looked wonderful and that there seemed to be no apparent long-term damage. Within twenty-four hours of waking up I was moved to a regular room, and exactly two days later I was told that I was strong enough to go home, as long as there was someone there to help me around the clock for a while, because of the multiple broken bones that I had suffered in the wreck. Between Ben, Mom, and Dad, I seriously doubt I'd have to worry about being left alone. The doctor did say I would have to come in for some physical therapy after the braces and cast came off. I could handle coming back in as long as my nights and most of my days were spent at home.

It was two days before Christmas and I was signing the release papers to get to leave the hospital. The nurse wheeled me out to the front entrance so that Ben could load me into his truck. I saw him waiting with Zoe standing by his side, smiling the biggest smile in my direction. I take it Ben had told her about my broken arm, leg, and crushed wrist because when she came up to me she very gently and timidly gave me the sweetest little hug I'd gotten in quite some time.

Ben picked me up and placed me in the passenger side of his truck. Zoe climbed up in the back behind me and my mom and dad were in my car behind us. They had offered to stay with me until I didn't need them anymore, just as I'd suspected they would do.

Ben drove slowly so that he wouldn't scare me. The trip that would normally take fifteen minutes took twenty-five. I thought it was very sweet of Ben to think about the fact that it might be rough on me getting into a vehicle for the first time after the wreck.

He asked me multiple times on the way home if I was all right. I assured him I felt fine, they had just given me some pain medication right before I left the hospital. I actually could feel no pain at that moment, partially thanks to the meds, and partially thanks to the fact that I was going to be ok and was with the man of my dreams.

As if he knew what I was thinking, he reached over and held my hand for the last half of the ride home. His soft, tender skin felt so good on my hand.

I thought all the way home, just as I had since I'd woken up from the coma, about telling Ben what happened to me while I was out. I don't know whether to believe it was a dream or if I really saw Laura when I was in my coma. I did know that it seemed very real, and I had a sense of calmness when I was with Ben, almost like Laura made it ok for me to be with him.

Ben got me settled into my house and then left to get Zoe ready for a Christmas play at their church that evening that she was going to be in. Mom and Dad were with me, though, almost to a smothering extent. They asked me every five minutes if I needed anything at all. I had eaten, had a glass of water next to the chair that I was in, and had the remote in my hand. Better than anything I had a new romance novel that Ben had gotten for me as a coming home gift, that I was already half through by the end of my first day at home.

The day before Christmas, Ben and Zoe came over and I was able to help them make a little bit of Christmas candy. I couldn't do much, since I had to remain sitting down because of my cast. Also, having one arm in a sling, limited my abilities in the kitchen. But there was no stopping my good hand from dipping candy into the melted chocolate and smothering it until they were coated with either milk chocolate or white chocolate. I also had no problems sampling the candy to make sure each batch was good.

I watched as Ben, Zoe, and Mom put together a gingerbread house as dad made some hot chocolate on the stove for us all to enjoy. I looked around my kitchen, seeing all the festive activities going on. The tree lit up in the living room and the gentle snow was falling outside my window. It was picture-perfect, and I was exactly where I was supposed to be. The Christmas candy tasted even better than usual and the decorations were more beautiful than ever. I knew that these things were no different than they were last year; but I was. I was happy, I was with the people I loved, and I was alive.

That night, as Ben and Zoe started to leave for home, I kissed Ben and gave Zoe a tight hug.

"Now Zoe, you go to bed as soon as you get home, darling. You know who will be visiting tonight," I winked at her, knowing I didn't have to remind her that Santa would be coming.

"I know Mia. I can't wait to see if I get the video game that I want," she said.

Ben winked at me before shutting the door and leaving me to go to bed myself.

As I lay in bed I couldn't help but think that there was nothing that Santa could bring me that would make me any happier than I already was. Thinking about my wonderful parents, that precious little Zoe, and the love of my life, Ben; I drifted off to sleep and enjoyed sweet dreams all night long.

I awoke the next morning, Christmas morning, to the smell of sausage cooking, brewed coffee, and pancakes on the griddle. The aroma reminded me of Christmas mornings when I was a child. I got up, pulled on a robe, and headed to the kitchen to join my mom and dad.

"Mom, that smells wonderful," I complimented her.

"Merry Christmas, Mia," she answered back. "And thank you very much."

"Merry Christmas," I told her in return, and turned to see my dad coming into the kitchen behind me.

"Hey Pumpkin, Merry Christmas," he said in a chipper voice.

I couldn't help but wonder why everyone was so cheerful and happy this morning. Maybe it was just the Christmas spirit flowing through us all. Maybe it was the fact that I had been okay from my wreck and had gotten home just in time for Christmas. Whatever it was, I was glad to see everyone so happy.

The phone rang across the kitchen and my mom answered it. She walked across the floor and handed it to me.

"Hello," I said knowing it was Ben, "and Merry Christmas."

"Merry Christmas to you my snow angel," Ben said. "How are you today?" he asked me.

"A little sore, but basically okay," I answered. "Is Zoe on cloud nine?" I questioned, knowing very well she was.

"She can hardly stand it. She goes from her video game, to the doll you got her, to the art kit she got. I had to make her come and eat breakfast," he laughed.

"When will you be over?" I asked him, not hardly being able to wait to see him today.

"Soon. It will be right after we go to church. Probably about lunchtime we should get out and can get over there," he said.

"I hate that I can't get out and come to church," I told him, feeling guilty even though I knew I was stuck inside for a while.

"Mia, you can't help it. Just turn on the TV and watch one of the Christmas services on there. Relax and we will be over in a few hours," he promised before hanging up.

I turned to face the table and saw my mom and dad looking across at me.

"You really love him don't you Mia," my mom asked me as my face started to blush a little.

"Yes, I do. He's the first man that has loved me for who I am. He has accepted my beliefs and actually shares my morals and values," I answered. "Now, enough talk about me, the food is getting cold, lets eat," I suggested hungry for the Christmas breakfast feast my mom had fixed.

We ate the wonderful food prepared that morning and enjoyed every minute of it. After breakfast, I washed up and changed into some decent clothes. I chose a pair of my favorite blue jeans, a green sweater, and I pulled my hair back into a loose ponytail. When I was finished I went back in to the living room to wait for Ben. I couldn't wait to give him the present I'd gotten him. Before my accident I had ordered tickets for him to go see one of the biggest rivalries in college basketball between his favorite team and another team from the same state. With a new coach that year, he was really excited, and had been into the games full-heartedly, so I knew he would love the present.

At exactly eleven thirty two I looked out of the window to see Ben's truck pulling into the driveway. He and Zoe got out, came to the front door, and rang the doorbell.

Mom went and let them in. I heard her greet them and wish them a Merry Christmas. She asked Zoe what Santa Claus had brought her, and I heard Zoe excitedly start naming off everything she got. As she was talking to my mom, I saw Ben come in through the doorway in jeans and a red button down shirt. He looked so handsome with his freshly shaven face and a smile that spread from ear to ear.

"Merry Christmas again, Mia darling," he said as he crossed the room to give me a tender kiss.

Zoe bounded into the living room before I could say anything else to Ben and plopped down on the couch next to me.

"Merry Christmas, sweetie," I said to her as I kissed her on top of the head. "Look at that pretty hair and that lovely dress. Did dad get you ready all by himself this morning?" I said, genuinely impressed by his new-found abilities.

"Yes, but it took him a long time," she said in return, Ben laughing at her.

"Well, don't keep me in suspense. What did Santa bring you?" I asked, acting like I didn't already know.

"I got my baby doll and my video game," she said excitedly. "And, I got some other stuff that I didn't even ask for, like an art kit," she added in.

"Wow, that is awesome. I want to be one of the first to get one of the art pieces that you create," I told her.

"Has my daddy given you your Christmas gift," she asked me excitedly.

"Zoe calm down and mind your manners," Ben told his daughter.

"Okay," Zoe whined.

"Why don't you go play your new video game or with your new baby doll with Mia's mom," he suggested, winking at my mom who was standing in the doorway.

"Yes, come on Zoe, we can play babies and I'll teach you how to change her diaper," my mother acted excited about playing with Ben's daughter.

"Okay," she agreed eagerly wanting to play with my mom. "And Daddy, don't forget to give Mia her present," she quickly demanded of his before exiting the room.

"This must be something good," I commented, seeing how excited Zoe was about it.

Ben laughed, "Zoe does get very excited easily," I admitted. "I hope you like it as much as she thinks you will."

"Can I give you mine first though," I asked him, eager to see his reaction to what I had gotten him.

"Sure thing," he said rubbing his hands together in excitement, just like a little child.

I handed him the box and he began unwrapping the green paper that had been neatly wrapped around the box with a red bow on top. When he pulled the tickets out of the box a smile spread all the way across his face. "Oh my gosh, Mia, are you kidding me," he said excitedly. "When did you get these? This is the game of the year!" he said, still staring at the tickets. "And these seats, they are the best," he added. "Thank you so much Mia, but, will you be able to go with me?" he asked.

"No, I want you to take a buddy with you, someone who will really enjoy the game with you. I like it just as well watching it on the TV," I assured him.

"Oh Mia, thanks a million. It's been forever since I have hung out with Bo, he will have a fit when I tell him about this," he said kissing me on the top of my head.

Ben stood up and started walking toward the hallway. I'll be right back with your gift, okay," he said to me as he walked out of sight. Within thirty seconds, he was coming back into the room carrying a blanket and basket. He spread out the blanket on the floor, and asked me to come set on it. He put a picnic basket in the middle with a candle and walked back out of the room. When he came back in he was carrying a vase of red lilies.

"Oh Ben, they are beautiful," I told him taking the flowers in my hand. "Where did you get red lilies this time of the year?" she asked me.

"I have my ways darling," he told me. Then he began, "Mia, do you remember the last time I gave you red lilies? It was the night we had a picnic in my backyard and I asked you to be my girlfriend," he said.

"How could I forget that?" I answered, thinking back to that starry summer night. Remembering him tell me that I stood out from all the other women like the white lily from the red ones.

He pulled out his hand from behind his back, holding another lily, this time a white calla lily.

"Well Mia, again I want to tell you that you still stand out from all the other women in the world for me. When you were lying in the hospital bed, I was hurting for you, like you were a piece of me. I realized I didn't want to live a day with out you in my life. Again Mia, with this white calla lily I have something very important to ask you," he went on. Ben got down on one knee right beside me and handed me the calla lily. At first, I didn't notice that there was something tied to stem of the calla lily. When I did, I looked closer to see what it was.

As my eyes came across the beautiful diamond ring that was gracefully hanging from the stem of the calla lily my legs felt weak and I started to cry.

"This time, *Cara Mia*, I want to ask you if you would do me the honor of being Mrs. Mia Allegra? Mia, will you marry me?" he asked, holding my hand, still down on one knee.

I looked at the ring and more tears started to flow down my cheeks. I was stunned, speechless.

"Oh no, your not going to say yes, are you? Is the ring wrong? Is it too soon?" he asked me.

"No Ben, I mean yes! YES, I will marry you!," I said happily. "I am just speechless. The ring is perfect; it is exactly what I would have picked. And the flower, you comparing the white lily to me," she added. "I have never loved anyone like I love you Ben, and I would love to spend the rest of my life with you. Oh my gosh, Zoe is going to be my stepdaughter. What will she think of this?" I asked Ben, not having to wait to find out.

Ben pointed toward the doorway and there stood my mom, dad, and Zoe, smiling at both of us.

"Oh Mia, you said yes! You are going to marry my daddy and be my mamma," she announced excitedly, beaming with happiness.

"Yes sweetie, that's what this means. I am going to be your step-mom," I commented, "just like your mom wanted me to be," I added quietly so that only Ben heard me.

He looked at me strangely, not knowing what I had meant by that statement. He didn't have time to ask me before my parents burst into the room, hugging and congratulating me. Mom wanted to start wedding planning immediately, and dad couldn't stop going on about how his little girl was finally going to get married and be happy. Ben watched lovingly from the side as I talked to my parents about the wedding.

The rest of my Christmas day went by so fast. I called LeAnne first; because of course she would have to be my matron of honor. She was thrilled at the news, although I had a feeling she had already known that this was going to happen. Next, I called some teachers from my school that were good friends of mine.

Ben and I had planned our wedding for May twenty-ninth, exactly one year from the day he asked me to be his girlfriend. I continued to heal, went back to work and of course spent much of my free time planning a beautiful church wedding. I kept everything as small and simple as I could. My arm and leg had healed nicely by the time the wedding day got here, and everything was going perfectly. My perfect day, the day I'd been dreaming about for years, was finally here.

Chapter 20

The Perfect Day

Our wedding day had finally gotten here. I woke up to a crisp sunny sky that morning. I got out of bed and pulled back the curtains so that the sunlight could shine through my bedroom window. I went into the bathroom to take a shower and get ready for the long wedding day that was ahead of me.

My mom and dad had gone home after my leg had healed in about mid February but had flown back in at the beginning of the week to help with wedding plans.

I walked into the kitchen to see my mom and dad already at the table enjoying a cup of coffee and a bagel.

"Good morning, Mia, its your big day!" my mom announced excitedly.

"Finally, I am tired of getting ready for it and ready to get it over with. I am super excited about the wedding, but more than anything I really can't wait to start my life as Mrs. Allegra," I admitted to my mother.

She gave me a kiss and told me I'd better eat and then get ready to go get my hair done at the salon.

The day quickly passed by and before I knew it I was standing in the bride's room at the church with my makeup and hair done and my beautiful dress on. I looked in the mirror at myself and couldn't believe this day had finally come. LeAnne peeked in the door to tell me it was time to go get in line to march in. I felt nervous and excited at the same time. I grabbed my bouquet of white calla lilies and walked out of the room.

I lined up behind my bridesmaids. First was my friend Stacie, who I also taught with, next in line was my sister-in-law Nell, after her was my matron of honor, LeAnne, and then my flower girl, Zoe. Zoe looked like a precious angel in her white dress and white halo of flowers around her hair.

The girls walked down the aisle one by one, and then it was my turn. The wedding march started, and the doors to the church opened wide. At the end of the long aisle I saw my handsome knight, the man I would spend the rest of my life with. He stood smiling with pure love and joy as I walked down the aisle with my dad toward him.

The church was full of friends and family who were there to witness this special day in Ben's and my lives. We were truly blessed to be in this beautiful church, surrounded by so much love. My father wiped a tear from the corner of his eye as he handed me off to Ben, shaking his hand and telling him to take good care of me.

The ceremony began and in no time it was time for us to say our vows. Ben had decided he wanted us to write our own vows, so going first; I recited the words that had come from my heart to let Ben know of my love and affection for him. Next, Ben said his vows and they went like this:

"Cara Mia, my darling, there are flowers that stand out, fine wine that is too good to drink. There are people who shine, places only people dream of visiting. However, none of these things can compare to you, my true love and friend. I vow to stay with you through all the ups and downs of life. I promise to raise my daughter and the kids that we will bring into this world together. You will forever and always be *Cara Mia*, My Darling," he finished, without leaving a dry eye in the church.

The priest announced us husband and wife, my new husband kissed me, and we started down the aisle as the whole congregation clapped and smiled.

As we were walking down the aisle arm in arm a soft wind gently swept through the church grazing both Ben's and my faces. I couldn't help but feel that it was Laura's presence blessing both Ben and I and the new life that we had just begun.